*87*

D0908370

FEB -- 1991

# Fatal Fortune

# MARIAN BABSON

# **Fatal Fortune**

A·THOMAS·DUNNE
BOOK

St. Martin's Press
New York

Library of Congress Cataloging-in-Publication Data

Babson, Marian.
    Fatal fortune / Marian Babson.
       p.    cm.
    "A Thomas Dunne book."
    ISBN 0-312-05428-9
    I. Title.
  PS3552.A25F38   1991
  813'.54—dc20                              90-48528
                                                   CIP

First published in Great Britain by William Collins Sons & Co. Limited

First U.S. Edition: February 1991
10 9 8 7 6 5 4 3 2 1

# CHAPTER 1

The newspapers invariably called it 'The North Shore Estate'. I suppose it was. To me, it was just home and it happened to be on the North Shore. The South Shore was largely *nouveau riche*; on the North Shore, a lot of the families were so old they weren't *riche* any more. Most of the great mansions had been sold off for use as schools or hotels; or, like the Hays Hammond Estate in Gloucester, turned into museums of a bygone era.

We were one of the few exceptions. I suppose it was natural for the media to be interested in us. For that and other reasons—like the news we made, for good or ill.

We had kept a low profile in the years since the big scandal, but now we were news again—despite ourselves. News we would rather not make, but news that was inevitable in the course of a long lifetime. The lifetime that was drawing to a close.

Horace (Buck) Bradstone was dying. The Old Buccaneer was fighting his last battle—the one we are all doomed to lose. It was just a question of time. But how he was fighting for every extra day!

'I don't know what he's hanging on for.' At least Vilma had had the sense to wait until her mother-in-law had left the room before voicing her opinion. 'He's seen everything, done everything and bought everything. He's had a good run for his money and he knows it. Why doesn't he just let go?'

'Please, dear.' My Cousin Everett divided an anxious glance between me and the ceiling. Upstairs, Buck Bradstone was not yet dead. There might be one last sting left in the scorpion—if a spy were to report to him.

'She doesn't mean that,' Everett told me nervously. 'She's

just exhausted. This has been a hard day.'

It had been one of Buck's better days. They could be worse than his bad days.

'We don't have any good days any more,' Vilma said. 'I don't know why he keeps hanging on.'

I did, but I didn't say anything.

'Life is a habit that's hard to break,' Everett reproved her. 'You might not be so willing to let go if it were you.'

'Try me!' Vilma snapped. 'If I were in that condition, I'd welcome a push!'

This time, they both looked at me in sudden fright. Too often, Vilma spoke before she thought. Too late, she realized that she could be in dire trouble if anyone took her seriously.

I didn't. Neither she nor Everett would do anything to hasten Buck's passing. Even if they dared, he was too well protected.

Nurse Helen watched him like a tigress, cosseting him, protecting him and—on his good days—flirting with him. It was private betting among the family that she had dreams of a deathbed marriage, with a grateful patient leaving everything to his devoted wife.

She didn't know Buck. It was family first, last and always with him. Or almost always.

I realized I was tense, waiting for the telephone to ring, measuring the distance I'd have to sprint, rehearsing the excuse I'd use as I snatched the telephone receiver out from under Ada's descending hand.

Vilma and Everett were still watching me, waiting for me to say something.

Aunt Florence re-entered, noted the uneasy silence, and looked from one to the other of us suspiciously. 'All right,' she said sharply. What is it?'

'Just a joke that fell a bit flat.' Everett spoke too quickly.

'Really?' Aunt Florence could guess who'd made the joke. Her gaze went unerringly towards her daughter-in-law.

Poor Vilma. She couldn't do anything right. Aunt

Florence would not have considered the best-bred Boston debutante worthy of her precious son; but she had expected him, at the very least, to choose one of them. When he had announced his intention of marrying a girl who was not only not a member of the Junior League, but had never even heard of them, she had thought it was the turn of her side of the family to make the scandal sheets.

However, the news that Everett Preston was marrying beneath him had burst upon the world with all the impact of a wet dishrag. Aunt Florence was the only person who cared—and, oh, how she cared! After a vain attempt to persuade them to elope quietly (with the Polish Church in Salem already booked, the wedding gown half-sewn, the invitations going out), she had settled down to a rear-guard action to minimize what she considered the damage. The fewest possible members of the family had been invited— and not all of us were able to go. Buck had had one of his first attacks and Ada and I had stayed home to look after him. It subsequently appeared that we had chosen the better part.

Aunt Florence had returned at midnight, pale, grim-faced, the hem of her blue lace dress ripped by an over-enthusiastic polka partner, with confetti and rice cascading from every part of her costume as she marched through the hall. She had gone straight to her room and remained there for three days, claiming a migraine. From that day to this, Vilma's appalling relatives had been a taboo subject.

I felt sorry for Vilma as she concentrated on her plate, her face flushed and rebellious. She had expected a more glamorous life as a rich man's wife. It had obviously never occurred to her that the rich had their troubles, too. There were some problems that even money couldn't solve.

'They're still camped down by the gatehouse,' Aunt Florence complained. 'I thought they'd have gone away by now. They've been there over a week. They weren't here nearly so long last time—' She broke off with a guilty look towards me.

'Last time was different,' I said quietly.

Last time, there was nothing to hang around for. After the initial sensation, there was the scramble of trying to get quotes and pictures from Buck and the family, then the whole thing had petered out. Not even a nine-days'-wonder, but the publicity juggernaut had rolled over us just the same, leaving us crushed if not broken. It would take more than that to break Buck. Tad had nearly succeeded.

'They won't go away this time,' Everett told his mother bitterly. 'They'll stay until—'

*Until it's all over.* We could all finish the sentence for him. We didn't. The unspoken words hung like a cloud over the dinner table.

We all became very busy with our meal again. That is, there was much play with knives and forks and pushing of food around plates, but no one actually ate very much.

Ada sniffed as she collected our plates. It could have been a comment on our lack of appetite; it could have been a moment of genuine emotion. Ada had been with the family for forty years, one way or another. If Buck were going to stage a deathbed wedding, there was little doubt in the family mind as to which woman ought to be the bride.

'Excuse me.' I pushed back my chair, unable to sit still any longer. I *had* to be near the telephone. 'I can't—I don't want anything else.'

'Not even coffee?' Ada tried to act affronted, but her heart wasn't in it.

'I'll come out to the kitchen and collect a cup.' I might be in for a long vigil, it would be as well to stay alert.

Ada nodded curtly and turned away just as another sniff escaped her. Emotion, then, not disapproval.

Vilma looked after me enviously as I left the table. She was trapped there until Everett and Aunt Florence decided to move. They were playing it out to the end, however, and settled back to wait for Ada to set the next course before them.

'I don't know—' Ada slammed the freezer lid down. 'You can say he's had a full life . . . a good run for his money . . . all that.' She rubbed the heel of her hand across her eyes. 'Just the same, it's always harder when one of the hell-raisers goes. They had so much life in them—'

'He's not gone yet.' I knew it was cold comfort I offered. It was just a matter of time.

'That's right!' She knew it, too. Her glance was bitter and she hit back instinctively—below the belt. 'It's just too bad he can't die a happier man. Everything he accomplished— turned to dust because his grandson brought shame and disgrace to the family name.'

'It wasn't Tad's fault! Not every man can be a hero.'

'No—but he doesn't have to be a traitor.'

'Tad was never a traitor.' But I said it wearily; the fire had gone out of my response long ago. I had countered the charge too often; from Buck, from the family, from friends, from the Press.

And now from Ada. I had thought she was on our side, she'd done so much of the raising of us after my parents had died in a boating accident. Perhaps that was why Ada was bitter. She must remember Tad as a little boy, clinging to his teddy-bear, lisping his prayers at night: 'And make me a good little boy . . .'

'He broke your grandfather's heart!'

Yes, that was the real charge against him. That was what Ada would never forgive—especially now.

'He broke all our hearts,' I said. 'Just remember—his own heart must have broken first.'

Tad had been raised to do his duty. He could not have failed without feeling the betrayal as much as any of us. His stern New England conscience would still be chiding him —probably in Buck's voice.

'He should be here,' Ada said harshly. 'No matter what, he should be here now.'

'I agree.' I could not say more without giving the game away, the last grim game we were all engaged in playing with a dying man.

I got a cup and saucer and helped myself to coffee from the coffee-making machine which was kept in constant use these days. I knew that I was not the only one to slip down during the long watches of the night and help myself to a cup or two. The caffeine didn't matter—none of us was doing much sleeping these nights, anyway.

'Hello, hello.' Nurse Helen appeared in the doorway and crossed to join me at the coffee machine. 'Great minds think the same, eh?' She helped herself to a cup, reached for the sugar, stopped herself, then shrugged and completed the gesture.

'It's been quite a day,' she said, almost defiantly, as she took two heaping spoonfuls. 'I need the energy.'

'He can be quite a handful,' I granted her. It didn't matter to us whether she cheated on her diet, but she seemed to feel some obscure need for absolution.

'You should have seen him in his prime,' Ada said.

'Yes . . . well . . .' Nurse Helen did not like to be reminded that she rarely saw her patients in their prime, nor even in the best of health. By the time she met them, they were on the downslide; if her ministrations were successful and they regained their health, they no longer needed her. It must be a thankless job and especially frustrating for a closet romantic like Nurse Helen. There are very few amorous exchanges across the bedpans and hypodermic needles.

'I'll just take this upstairs.' She was not prepared to linger and cross swords with Ada. 'I'm afraid we're due for a restless night.'

'She's still in there trying,' I said, as soon as she was safely out of earshot. 'Always fresh lipstick and not a hair out of place.'

'I'll worry when her hair is mussed and her lipstick smeared.' Ada began stripping the foil coverings from individual frozen portions of parfait. 'You want any of this ice-cream or not?'

'Not.' All I wanted was to get back to the study and wait for that telephone call. Surely it must come at any minute now. What was the time difference between Massachusetts and Sweden . . .?

'You're up to something, don't think I don't know it!'

There was no answer to that. She knew me too well. I smiled noncommittally and headed for the door.

'I just hope you know what you're doing!' she shot after me.

'So do I.'

The family were still safely anchored in the dining-room and I slipped past noiselessly. The study looked out to sea; it was dark and cool. I crossed to the window and stood sipping my coffee. The sky was darkening rapidly, whitecaps foamed on the crest of the waves. The tide was coming in, it splashed restlessly against the rocks below. Buck had always loved the sound of the surging tide; he'd stand here by the open window, or out on the terrace, looking down as the waves crept up the cliff. Before he realized how much it upset me when I was a child, he used to say, 'Some day I'll go out on the ebb tide, my girl. It carries the journeying spirit home . . .'

I turned away abruptly. The room was too dark, my vision was blurring. Lights. I snapped on the floor lamp, the desk lamp, the lamp beside the big leather chair by the bookcase, but the room still seemed dark.

I slumped into the desk chair and kept sipping at my coffee. Perhaps it had been a mistake not to put some brandy in it.

The telephone startled me, a brown blob spilled on to the desk blotter and sank into it in a widening stain. I set down my cup and picked up the receiver, cutting off the second ring. With luck, no one might have heard it.

'Hello . . .? Hello . . .?' I seemed to speak into an echoing void, a sense of distance throbbed along the open wire. This was the call I had been waiting for. 'Hello . . .?'

'Hello . . . I wish to speak to Miss Hope Bradstone, please . . .'

'Yes, I'm Hope Bradstone. What is it? *Who* is it?' This was not the voice I had expected to hear. It was faint, thready, female.

'You are Hope? How do you do? This is Inga. Inga . . . your sister-in-law . . .'

'Inga, hello. How nice to meet you—well, sort of meet. How are you? How's my nephew? How's . . . Tad?'

'I have read your letter . . .'

'Tad's letter? I mean, my letter to Tad?'

'That is right. He was not here. I waited and waited. And then I thought it might be important to answer. It said "Urgent" . . .'

'Yes, that's all right.' She seemed to need reassurance. 'But where's Tad?'

'He is away on business.' She sounded more sure of herself. 'When he did not come back . . . on schedule . . . I opened the letter and read it . . .'

'Yes, yes, that's all right, Inga. I understand. That is, I don't *quite* understand. When will Tad be back? Can't you get in touch with him? This really is very important.'

'Yes, that is why I ring now. Very important. I must speak to you . . .'

'Yes, go ahead.' Only the strange whistling of space and distance came to me. With a sinking feeling, I tried again. She seemed to require endless prodding. 'We're speaking now, Inga. What did you want to say?'

'No . . . we cannot talk like this. I must see you.' Suddenly her voice firmed. 'It is for Tad, for Jan-Carl. It is, maybe, life or death. Can you come?'

'Wait a minute.' I had begun to feel slightly dizzy, as

though a chasm had suddenly opened at my feet and the whistling wind was trying to suck me down into it. 'What do you mean? Come where? Not to Sweden? Not now!'

'Now! Soon! Immediately! If you leave tonight, you can be here in the morning. But not Sweden. It is not safe there. I have taken Jan-Carl away where they cannot find us. We are not in Sweden now.'

'Who can't find you? Inga, where are you? What's going on? What's happened to Tad?'

'I do not know. We are in Germany. Maybe this is not safe, either, but it is where I have last heard from him. I try to find him.'

'You mean Tad is missing—?' Just in time, I bit down on the bitter word '*again*'.

'It is not like that.' She sensed what I had nearly said. 'He would not have left us. He would not desert those who depended on him.'

We had thought that once.

'No! No!' My silence seemed to unnerve her. 'It is trouble. Bad trouble. But I do not know what kind. He did not tell me anything. He said the less I knew, the better. But now he is gone—' Her voice broke. 'And I know nothing. Not even where to look for him.'

'But you're in Germany now,' I reminded her. 'Where-abouts in Germany? What city? Town?'

'It does not matter. I shall not be here long. I—I travel.'

'Inga,' I said urgently. 'Come over here. *You* can be *here* in the morning. Never mind Tad for the moment. Come here—and bring Jan-Carl with you.'

'I cannot. But, yes, Jan-Carl should be there. A man has a right to see his great-grandson before he dies. And it will be better for Jan-Carl to go where he will be safe.'

'Safe? Inga—'

'I stay here. I must be where Tad can find me. You must come and get Jan-Carl.'

'Inga, I can't leave the country now. Don't you understand? My grandfather is dying. That was why I was trying to reach Tad. He—all of you—must come before it's too late.'

'It is impossible. You must come here.'

'Inga, be sensible. You won't even tell me where you are. How can I go there?'

'I will tell you where we will meet. You can take a plane and be here in the morning. There is a small hotel in Brussels —the *Poisson d'Or* in the *Rue de Morel*, near the *Grand Place*. It is where we had our honeymoon. We will meet you there. Then you can take Jan-Carl home with you. It will be better for him.'

'Inga, it's impossible! Can't I make you understand—?' But even as I protested, my hand jotted down the address on the scratch pad beside the telephone.

'It is you who do not understand.' Her voice held all the stubbornness traditionally associated with the Swedish, but abruptly, it broke. 'Whatever happens, my son must live!'

'Why shouldn't he live?' The despair and terror in that suddenly ragged voice infected me. 'Inga, what are you trying to tell me? Is . . . is Jan-Carl ill? Does he need medical treatment?'

'The *Poisson d'Or*,' she repeated urgently. 'You must be there tomorrow. I cannot speak more. Already, they may —' She broke off.

'Inga, wait! Don't hang up! Are you still there?'

'I must go. It is not safe. But, please, you must come for Jan-Carl. I beg. There is no one else to help us.'

'Inga, listen. I'll make arrangements. I'll have someone there at the *Poisson d'Or* to collect Jan-Carl and bring him over here.'

'No! I trust no one else! You must come yourself. I have seen your pictures, read your letters. I do not trust my son to—' her voice had gone as cold as the Nordic fjords. 'I do not trust my son to . . . an emissary!'

'Inga, are you worried about kidnapping?' It had always

been Buck's secret dread that someone would try it with one of us. Tad, Everett and I had made it through to adulthood safely, but now there was a new generation vulnerable. Was someone plotting one last assault on Buck's fortune before it was disseminated to the various heirs?

'Worse . . . worse . . .' she wailed. 'I explain tomorrow. I see you then.'

'But, Inga—' It was too late. The connection was broken.


## CHAPTER 2

There was barely time to think. If I was going, I would have to get to Logan Airport before the last International flight left for the night. It didn't actually matter which one I caught; once in Europe, I could connect with a flight to Belgium easily enough.

Was I going? This was all I needed: an international crisis in the midst of the worst domestic crisis it was possible to face. If I left now and Buck died while I was gone, I would never forgive myself. If I didn't go and something terrible happened to Jan-Carl I would never forgive myself, either. No matter what I did, it was a no-win situation for me.

Unless . . . Buck had been hanging on for weeks now. He was even slightly better today. It had been months since the doctor told us, 'It could be any day now.' Buck was fighting the good fight, but all of us could see that his strength was diminishing daily, perhaps hourly, now. But he was tough . . . determined . . .

How long could it take? Literally, a flying trip to Europe. Time and distance weren't what they had been in Buck's heyday. As Inga had said, I could be there in the morning. Another few hours to meet up with Inga and collect Jan-Carl, perhaps pick up Concorde at Paris for the flight back . . . it could be done in twenty-four hours or so.

Surely, Buck would last another twenty-four hours.

I paused outside Buck's door, one hand on the doorknob, listening. There was silence inside the room. A good sign . . . probably. It didn't make much noise just to lie there and breathe . . . or die.

I turned the knob and opened the door a crack. There was no hiss of the oxygen cylinder to be heard. Another hopeful sign. Buck's good day hadn't taken too much out of him, after all.

The same couldn't be said for Nurse Helen. She slumped in the big wing chair, her paperback romance in danger of sliding off her lap and waking both her and her patient as it hit the floor.

I stepped into the room and closed the door silently behind me. She was instantly awake; a good nurse, despite all her faults.

'Miss Bradstone—what are you doing here?' She was on the defensive, furious at being caught dozing, even for a second. 'You shouldn't be disturbing your grandfather at this hour.'

If anyone was going to disturb him, she was. She rushed over and began fussing unnecessarily with the tray at his bedside.

'I'm sorry.' She had to be placated; we needed her. 'I didn't mean to disturb Buck. I just wanted to see him for a minute.'

'Well, there he is.' She waved at his recumbent form. 'Having a nice peaceful rest after a long day.' She waited for me to look my fill and leave.

'I'm sorry, Nurse Helen, I know you've had a long day, too, but do you think you could get me a cup of coffee? And get another one for yourself. I'll stay here and watch him until you get back.'

She'd have loved to refuse, but didn't quite dare. The family of the patient had some rights, however much the nurse on duty might feel that the sickroom was hers alone.

'Just don't disturb him.' She walked towards the door, trying to look as though it had been her own idea. 'He needs his sleep.'

'I won't wake him.' Buck awake was the last thing I wanted. I kept smiling and stood my ground until the door closed behind her. I gave it a count of ten and then dashed for the desk.

I knew what I was looking for; it was an open secret in the family. I slid the top left-hand drawer all the way out and set it down on the carpet, then reached in to get at the secret compartment at the back.

Damn! The tiny key wasn't in the lock. Sometimes it was, sometimes it wasn't, depending on how trusting Buck was feeling at the time. With Nurse Helen around, I didn't blame him for being in a mistrustful mood.

The back of my neck suddenly prickled and I knew I was being watched. I straightened up and swung to face the door, formulating an excuse for Nurse Helen as I met her accusing eyes. The doorway was empty; the door still closed. More slowly, I turned to face the bed.

'That's right,' I said to Buck. 'I'm rifling your desk. I'm after the Emergency Fund.' Buck had always kept a float of at least five thousand dollars in cash in the secret compartment. He believed that you never knew when you might need to travel suddenly and it behoved you to have enough cash on hand to get you anywhere in the world you might want to be and keep you for a few days while currency formalities were worked out with the relevant authorities. It was an arrangement that had stood him in good stead in his day; now it was my turn to take advantage of it.

'Where's the key?' He hadn't spoken, but the glint of amusement in his eyes encouraged me. 'I wouldn't like to break that nice little lock.'

He shook his head. I wasn't going to get away with it as easily as that. He raised an inquiring eyebrow.

'I promise you, it's an emergency.'

He nodded acknowledgement. He knew me well enough to trust me in that regard. I wouldn't just be taking advantage of his illness. If I was after the Emergency Fund, then I had a reason—a good reason. At least, one that I thought was good. His opinion might be different.

'Lock . . .' he whispered. His eyes turned towards the door, finishing the sentence for him. We didn't need Nurse Helen bursting in to interrupt a private conference.

'Yes, of course.' I crossed to the door and turned the key in the lock, hoping we could be finished before she returned. She wouldn't take kindly to being locked out of her own workroom.

Buck cocked an eyebrow again as I turned to face him. He waited.

'I need a couple of thousand,' I told him. 'I have to fly to Brussels tonight.'

He didn't need to waste his breath speaking, his expression was eloquent.

'I shan't be gone long. Twenty-four hours or so. I'll be back before you know I've gone. And I'll bring Jan-Carl with me.'

'Jan-Carl . . .?' The whisper was so faint I could barely hear him.

'Don't try to pretend you don't know who Jan-Carl is. Tad's son. My nephew. Your great-grandson.'

'Tad . . .' He shook his head, frowning. 'Dead . . . to me.'

'Maybe so, but Jan-Carl is alive and he needs us. Whatever Tad has or hasn't done, you can't take it out on the child. He's your own flesh and blood. *Our* blood. He belongs here with the family—and I'm going to get him and bring him back. I'd like to do it with your blessing—but I'm going to do it, anyway.'

Something dangerously close to a smile flickered on his lips. Opposition had always been the breath of life to him.

I went back to the desk and rattled the little door standing between me and the money I needed. It held firm, too firm.

I took off my shoe and gave the lock a couple of preliminary taps.

'I don't want to break it, but if I have to . . .'

His eyes were closed, one hand beneath his pillow. Had he fallen asleep again? Or . . . was the excitement too much for him?

'Miss Bradstone!' There was a thump at the bedroom door, the doorknob rattled. 'Miss Bradstone, is anything wrong? I can't open the door. Miss Bradstone!'

'She's back already—blast her! Why can't she mind her own business?' I aimed the shoe at the compartment door for a final desperate assault.

'Hope . . .' The whisper was so faint I might have missed it. I turned, but his eyes were closed, his face pale and still. His hand had moved from beneath the pillow, though. It hung over the side of the bed and there below it was the tiny key to the secret compartment.

'Miss Bradstone! Miss Bradstone!' Nurse Helen was pounding on the door now. She'd have everyone in the house up here if she didn't stop.

'Just a moment, Nurse,' I called. 'I can't come now. I—I'll drop him.'

'Oh!' The pounding stopped abruptly, the doorknob began twisting again. 'What's going on? What are you doing to him?'

'Just a moment.' Buck was snorting with amusement as I snatched up the key, dashed to the desk and grabbed the folder from the secret compartment. I left the key in the lock and jammed the concealing outer drawer back into place.

Then I rushed to unlock the door before Nurse Helen had a fit out there. Just before I opened it, I looked again at Buck. He was so still again. Should I have involved him in this? Had the excitement drained away yet more of the rapidly emptying pool of energy and strength?

'Buck?' I moved closer to the bed. 'Are you still . . . awake? Thank you. I'll be back soon. You'll see Jan-Carl.'

His eyes opened suddenly. He stared at me commandingly, his lips moved. Another faint, fading whisper: '*Hurry* . . .'

Ada was still in the kitchen, relieving her feelings by crashing the dinner dishes around in the sink. She never bothered with the dish-washer when she was really upset. It hadn't been used for weeks now.

'*Now* what?' She became aware that someone was watching her and whirled on me. The dish she was holding slammed against the side of the sink and a few chips went flying.

'I was just wondering . . .' I tried to sound casual, although I knew it wouldn't fool her. 'Remember that blonde wig the live-in maid left behind when she got a job in the city. Any idea what ever happened to it? I mean, it's still around somewhere, isn't it?'

'You mean to tell me—' She hurled the dish back into the soapy water—'you're worrying about a wig at a time like this? What do you want to know for?'

'I just wondered where it was. I got to thinking about it, and I—' I broke off. This was getting too implausible and I wasn't fooling her for a minute. I should have known better than to try.

'Go on,' she jeered. 'The trouble we've got on our hands right now and all you can think about is an old wig the hired girl left behind. Tell me another!'

'All right.' I gave up. 'I have to go somewhere. On business. I thought the best way of getting past the reporters at the gate would be to, sort of, disguise myself. No one would recognize me in that blonde wig.'

'They wouldn't, and that's a fact. You might attract a different kind of attention, though. They can't see many blonde sheep driving a car.' But she was drying her hands and a thoughtful look had come over her face. 'What sort of business?'

'Never you mind.' That was what she used to say to us when we were children. I should have known I wasn't going to get away with that one, either.

'Stop that! I'm not a fool. I can see you've dipped into the Emergency Fund. That means you're going some distance. Where? And . . . how long will you be gone?'

'Well . . .' I'd forgotten I was still holding the tell-tale folder and that Ada knew the tale. She had permission herself to dip into the Emergency Fund—not that she had ever availed herself of the privilege. 'It's an emergency. It really is.'

'I'm not questioning that. You've got enough sense to know what's what. I want to know it, too.'

'Europe . . .' I winced as I said it; it sounded so awful, so far away, as though I were deserting a lost cause. 'But I have to—and I'll be back as fast as I can. It shouldn't take more than a day, or a day-and-a-half. It's not a pleasure trip.'

'I'm not stupid enough to imagine it was. Stop apologizing. It's—' Ada looked over her shoulder instinctively to make certain we were still alone and lowered her voice. 'It's Tad, I suppose.'

'In a way.' I had always been aware that she had known I had kept in sporadic touch with Tad. Occasionally one of his letters had been thrust back into its envelope upside-down. I had never tried to hide the rare letters. In fact, I had made a point of leaving each new one in plain view on my dressing-table for a few days before putting it away with the others. Ada had been like a mother to us both and she had the right to read Tad's news—even though she would never admit she had. She relayed the news to Buck, I suspected, so that he could remain aloof and unforgiving, but not unknowing. A couple of years ago there had been a batch of photographs of Inga and Jan-Carl—and one of them had disappeared permanently. All that week, Buck had walked with a new spring in his step.

'What way? Either it is, or it isn't. And you wouldn't leave your grandfather at a time like this if it wasn't. You're not thinking of dragging Tad back for some sort of deathbed reconciliation, are you? It won't work. Buck may be dying, but he hasn't gone soft.'

'I can't bring Tad back with me—he's disappeared.'

'Disappeared?'

'That's what Inga said. That was her on the telephone a little while ago.'

'I knew you were up to something!' Ada nodded. 'So what are you going over for now? Think you can find him?'

'I'm not even going to look. There—there isn't time. I'm going to get Jan-Carl. Buck has no quarrel with him—and he belongs here with us. He's a Bradstone.'

'Right!' Ada's eyes gleamed. 'And about time, too. I'll get the old nursery ready. He's about seven years old now, isn't he?' The dishes forgotten, she started for the door.

'First,' I reminded her, 'I need that wig. I don't want a horde of reporters following me to the airport.'

'I'll get it. And you'd better borrow my old car. No one seeing you in that and the wig would think it was anything more than Maid's Night Out. You can leave the car at the airport and pick it up when you get back. If anybody should steal it meantime, I'll turn a profit on the insurance.'

She was right. It was one of the little independences that had driven Buck mad—yet, at the same time, made him respect her more. He had offered countless times to buy her a new expensive car, any make, any model; the choice was to be hers.

She had chosen to pay for her own car out of her own salary, cars that were so old they weren't even second-hand. Fifth- or sixth-hand, more likely. She'd driven them right into the ground and, despite Buck's pleas and protests, promptly bought another one just as rundown and cheap.

No one seeing me in the current jalopy would imagine I

was a member of the family. With that and the wig, I should have no trouble getting past the death watch outside the gatehouse.

## CHAPTER 3

Russ would have noticed the automobile even if it hadn't nearly run him down. You didn't see many old rattletraps like that in this affluent country. In the Third World countries where he had spent so much time, they were the norm.

He nearly dropped the typewriter as he leaped out of the way, barking his shin on the mudguard of one of the parked cars.

The driver of the rattletrap hadn't even noticed him. Any accident would have been his own fault; he was looking in the wrong direction for traffic. Too busy brooding over his private concerns, he had let dangerous automatic reflexes take over. They were dangerous because they were still attuned to the world he had left behind.

He was too newly arrived, after being too long away. He shouldn't be out without a keeper.

So, where was Artie?

He had telephoned the newspaper office after clearing Customs and Immigration and been assured that Artie was on the way to pick him up with a car. He should be telephoning the office again and demanding to know the whereabouts of Artie and that car. He should be thinking over the book he planned to write about those lost years and all the experiences he wished he had not had. He should be dreaming about the reunions with dear ones—those he had remaining—and worrying about picking up the threads again in an existence that had so often in the past years seemed to have been but a dream.

He should not be staring at a lady driver because she

looked strangely familiar. Strange being, perhaps, the operative word. How could anyone imagine that straw, even blonde straw, added anything to her appearance? Strange, the ways of Western women.

Because he had spent so many months in the drablands, he watched her in fascination as she locked the car and headed purposefully for Terminal B. Was orange the fashionable colour for lipstick at the moment?

No. He noticed the other women. Most of them wore no lipstick at all. Sensible, if they were boarding a night flight where no one was going to pay any particular attention to them. In the morning, just before landing, they could put on their make-up, attend to their hairdos, and generally put on whatever cosmetic armour would enable them to face a new day in another country.

Automatically, he had followed her into the Terminal, still fretting over that imagined likeness to someone he had known in an American past he could barely remember. What did it matter if a passable young woman chose to travel in an ancient and unbecoming wig.

That was it. A wig. Visualize her without that and she immediately became younger and more attractive and—almost—identifiable. The familiarity teased at his consciousness. She was someone he had known in the past. Here in New England, before his foreign assignments. A story?

Recognition was coming closer. She was older, lots older. So was he. They had met—no, collided. No love lost between them. That was it. Nothing social, strictly business. She had been part of a story . . . a child on the periphery of a big story. A . . . scandal?

He moved closer as the line she had joined shuffled forward towards the Reservations Desk. She was deep in her own thoughts, not noticing that she was under observation. Good. If he could just get close enough, he might be able to hear something, catch a glimpse of her credit card, learn her name and destination. He *knew* her, she was *someone*, one of the people who made the news. The conviction was strong in him now. If he just followed her, she would lead him to a major story, perhaps the newsbeat of his life. She was . . .

Never mind her, he was mad! What was he doing? One hand already reaching for his credit card as he slid into the line behind her, one corner of his mind occupied with toting up his status: his passport still had a month to run before renewal; he had about seventy-five dollars in US cash, one hundred and fifty dollars in travellers cheques and about another hundred dollars' worth of assorted European currencies. Not nearly enough to take off on a wild goose chase after some skirt who might or might not lead him to that Shangri-La of ambition: the exclusive story which would etch his name indelibly on the American consciousness.

His long tour of foreign duty was over, and not before time. He was in danger of losing touch with his roots, his public and—worse—the point of view of his newspaper. There had already been intimations in the most recent editorial communications. It was time he settled down to a spell of local duty and relearned the imperatives of New England life.

Reviving a local scandal would make as good a start as any. What *had* she—or someone near her—done in that distant barely-remembered past?

She was paying in cash. His antennæ quivered. That was part of it; there had been money involved—plenty of it. A family full of it. Family . . . identification was coming closer.

The reservations clerk was filling out her ticket now and he craned forward to try to read it. He needed to know what destination to ask for when his turn came. 'I'm following that girl' was not to be recommended as an opening gambit when discussing a destination.

Neither was leaning on the woman in front of him.

'Get offa me, you lousy pervert!' she snarled.

Everyone turned to stare at him. The clerk lifted her head

and looked at him thoughtfully, then made a note on a jotting pad, probably to warn the stewardess on his flight of a possible troublemaker aboard.

'I'm sorry,' he apologized to the belligerent woman glaring at him. 'I slipped.'

'Yeah, sure. That's what they all say!'

The girl turned back to the clerk, still holding her half-counted money, obviously dismissing him from her thoughts. But his thoughts suddenly clicked into place: that profile, in conjunction with all that cash.

The Bradstone heiress!

'Just don't try nothing more—that's all I got to say!' With a final glare, the heavy middle-aged woman in front turned her back on him.

He didn't even hear her. Memories were flooding back. The Bradstones. Old Buck Bradstone, last incarnation of the Robber Barons, with that huge estate on the North Shore. All those millions and all that family pride.

And his family had let the old boy down. At least, the one member of it he had depended on most; the young boy to whom he had looked for the continuance of the name. The grandson—Tom? Ted? Tad—that was it. Short for Thaddeus. A good name, Thaddeus Bradstone, but it had taken more living up to than the kid was capable of.

Just a kid in those days. What—eighteen? Nineteen? Too young—hell, they were all too young—to face the horrors of Vietnam. Swept from his cosseted life to a steaming jungle hell. And all because of Old Buck's macho pride. He'd taken the kid out of college and volunteered him for the Draft. While other, more realistic, wealthy families were sending their sons across the Canadian border, the old monster had called a Press Conference and made a song and dance about Patriotism—with a capital P—and the Duty owed to one's Country. Too old to go to war himself, Buck Bradstone had rashly offered up his only grandson on the altar of America the Beautiful and stood by with a beneficent smile on his face while the kid was whisked off to Vietnam the Ugly, the Nightmare, the war that should never have happened. He had only himself to blame for what had followed.

Give the kid credit, he had stuck it out for over a year. Against what odds could only be guessed. He'd been in the thick of the fighting—hadn't they all?—seen his friends blown away beside him, watched the horrors perpetrated by both sides, stumbled through a world of chaos and bloodshed until—like others before and after him—he had snapped.

Apart from Buck Bradstone, could anyone really blame the kid for deserting?

Hope! That was her name: Hope Bradstone. Although she hadn't looked very hopeful in those days, trailing behind her grandfather, a pale childish shadow, as he denounced her big brother, disinherited him, and forbade anyone ever to speak his name again. Which was as good a way as any of dodging awkward questions when the media converged on his mansion and laid siege to his gates.

Buck Bradstone had won out, of course. News never stopped happening and he had been able to hole up behind those granite walls until a more urgent scandal had superseded his own. One by one, the reporters at his gates had been called away to more pressing assignments. Russ himself had been one of the last to leave and so he had often glimpsed that pale fine-boned profile sliding past behind the windows of her grandfather's Cadillac as the chauffeur ferried her back and forth to her exclusive Day School.

Small wonder that he had not recognized her immediately behind the wheel of that ancient flivver; amazing that he had spotted her at all.

Or perhaps not so amazing. Call it luck, call it intuition, he'd always had that ability to spot the oddity that could lead to a story. Sometimes, just a wistful column; sometimes, headlines.

This time?

She turned away from the counter, holding a ticket folder in the Sabena Airline colours, and moved towards the departure lounge. The line shuffled forward.

'There you are!' Artie appeared beside him. 'What the hell are you doing in this line? I've been waiting for you outside. Come on, let's get going! I haven't got all night.'

'You have now,' Russ said. 'I'm not staying.'

'Huh?'

'Here, take the typewriter. And here's the ticket for my luggage, I'll just keep my flight bag. And listen, Artie, how much money have you got on you?'

'Now wait a minute. I'm taking Betty out tonight after I dump you off at the paper. It's bad enough, traffic making me so late—'

'Good, then you should have plenty to spare.'

''I can't spare a cent—' But Artie, well-trained, was already fumbling for his wallet. 'Betty's a very expensive woman—and old-fashioned. She lets me pick up the check every time.'

'Then it's time you started changing that.' Russ deftly plucked the wallet from Artie's fingers and began riffling through it, removing the currency. 'My need is greater than hers.'

'Hey—stop that!' Artie snatched ineffectually at his wallet. 'What the hell do you think you're doing?'

'Providing for emergencies—and we're in the middle of one right now, in case you hadn't noticed.' Of course, Artie hadn't noticed; that was why he was still on a local beat, running errands for the management. His own preoccupations had always loomed larger than the overall picture.

'Give that back! I can't take Betty out on an empty wallet. She'd never speak to me again!'

'It would be the best thing for you, my boy.' Russ tucked the wad of bills into his own wallet. 'Go and find yourself a good, liberated woman, who'll stand her share of the expenses.'

'You're jet-lagged outa your mind! Give that back!'

'So, he's a thief, too!' The woman just in front had finished her business at the desk while they squabbled. 'I'm not surprised. You want me to get a cop for you while you hang on to him?'

'That's not a bad idea.' Artie snatched back the now empty wallet and glared at Russ.

'Just a private dispute between friends, madam.' Russ smiled falsely at the woman. 'No cause for alarm.'

'People like you are the biggest cause for alarm there is.'

'She's got a point there,' Artie said bitterly.

'Oh, er—' Russ had reached the desk. 'A ticket to Brussels, please. One way.'

'One way? You just got back. You're crazy!' Artie pulled a handkerchief from his pocket and wiped his forehead. A couple of dollar bills fluttered to the floor.

'Ah-ah, holding out on me!' Russ dived and scooped them up before Artie could move.

'Leave me something,' Artie moaned. 'Suppose I run out of gas on the way back?'

'Use your credit card.' Russ flourished his own at the reservations clerk.

'You mean you're not going to take that, too?'

'Stop complaining, I'm going to pay you back.'

'When? You just bought a one-way ticket.'

'That's three lucky people tonight,' the girl commented, writing out his ticket. 'If the Brussels flight hadn't been delayed, you would never have made it.' She appeared unconcerned by Artie's grumbling, obviously accustomed to last-minute panic raids on the funds of family and friends by travellers who suddenly worried about having enough currency.

'I guess it's just my lucky night,' Russ said. How lucky, remained to be seen. He could have wished that the belligerent woman wasn't bound for Brussels, too. Anyway— he looked on the bright side—if Fate were so unkind as to

seat them together, she could be depended on to demand to
have her seat changed. He was not one of her favourite
people.

'What is all this?' Artie demanded. 'I can't go back to the
paper and tell them you took one look at America and got
right straight back on a plane. They're going to want a
better explanation than that. If you've got one.'

'Thank you.' Russ took the ticket the girl held out to him.

'They'll start boarding any minute now,' she warned him.

'Come on.' Russ moved towards the parking lot, Artie
floundering in his wake. 'We can't talk here.'

'Okay,' Artie said, as they got out of earshot. 'What the
hell's bitten you?'

'You didn't notice that girl at all, did you?'

'What girl? Not your special friend? I couldn't miss her.
But if you're calling her a girl, you've been away from
civilization too long.'

'Not her, the one in front of her. Wearing the yellow floor
mop.'

'Don't try to tell me it was love at first sight. I'll believe
a lot but—'

'Forget it.' They had reached Artie's car and Russ waited
for him to unlock it. 'Tell me, do you remember the Bradstone scandal?'

'Bradstone? Like in old Buck Bradstone? He's dying.
What scandal? I'll look it up in the morgue. They should
have all the clippings. Something to spice up the obituary
notice, eh?'

'Dying . . . you mean right now?'

'Failing for most of the summer. We're expecting the
announcement any minute. They say *Time* and *Newsweek*
have special features ready to roll.'

'Dying. Then why is his granddaughter flying off to
Europe at a time like this?'

'Hey—you think it's another one like that great Back Bay
scandal?' Artie might not remember much about wars, but

he was strong on sex scandals. 'Remember that broad from Beacon Hill who stabbed her lover to death, locked the body in a closet and flew to Europe? She was very pregnant at the time, too. Some kind of debutante.'

'A failed debutante, I'd say. No, it won't be anything like that.'

'How do you know? Maybe she's just given the Old Boy a push.'

'Why bother when it's just a matter of time, anyway? Not worth the risk and she's got plenty of time.'

'Yeah . . .' Artie hated to let go of a juicy theory. 'You sure you don't want the typewriter?'

'No, I don't think I'll be gone that long. I'll give it a couple of days and, if nothing pans out, I'll be back by the end of the week.' The girl had been carrying just a single piece of cabin luggage, some sort of holdall. You could pack quite a lot into them, but not enough for any extended stay. Perhaps she intended to buy a wardrobe *en route*, but he doubted it. She wouldn't want to be away from her grandfather for long at a time like this. The Bradstones were very strong on Family. Unless, of course, someone had done something to disgrace the family.

Was that it? Had she blotted the family escutcheon in some way and been found out at the last minute? Had she, too, been disowned and sent to join her brother in exile?

'You know,' Artie said, 'I think I'll drive down to the North Shore in the morning. Have a look around. You never know what you might pick up . . .'


CHAPTER 4


The *Poisson d'Or* was in a tiny winding side street in the old part of the city. Cobblestones, ancient streetlamps, narrow pavements—where there were pavements at all—and dark, secretive houses with heavy net curtains drawn tight to shut out any prying gaze. It was very much off the beaten track; no tourist would find the way here except by accident and the unwelcoming atmosphere would ensure a hasty retreat.

The taxi drew up in front of a recessed doorway whose flanking shrubbery indicated that it might possibly be open to the public. Above the door faint gilt lettering could just be discerned. The Poisson d'Or—journey's end.

I had to pay the taxi-driver in American currency, recklessly thrusting too much at him to stifle any complaints he might make about the current rate of exchange. He accepted it with a heavy sigh, but drove off rapidly before I could think it over and perhaps change my mind.

The lobby was tiny, only a small reception desk in the corner identifying it as a lobby rather than some sort of vestibule. Firmly closed doors obviously gave on to other rooms, but there were no signs to suggest which rooms. There was nothing wrong with my reception, however.

'Ah, yes, Miss Bradstone.' Thank heavens she spoke English. 'We have your reservations. You and your sister have a family accommodation, that is correct?'

'If that's what my—my sister reserved.' Presumably, Inga knew more about what she was doing than I did. 'Has she arrived yet?'

'We do not expect her until this evening. Your passport, please.'

Reluctantly, I handed it over. I always hate letting it out of my grasp. I can't lose the faint uneasy feeling that someone will whisk it away and I'll never see it again and be left stranded in a foreign land with no protection at all. I knew it was just another manifestation of Travellers' Twitch, that strange malady that descends on tourists and keeps them constantly checking their documents and valuables. Right now, I longed to get to my 'family accommodation—' whatever that might be—and lie down and count my currency.

That taxi-driver had looked altogether too happy as he had
driven off.

Madame glared at my passport as though I had just
forged it myself and the ink was still wet. Distrustfully,
she copied details down on to her hotel registration form.
Finally, she stared long and hard at my passport photo,
then raised her hard cold eyes to my face and arched an
eyebrow at me.

That wretched wig! It had not been in the best of shape
when Ada and I had unearthed it in the storeroom. We had
attacked it with styling mousse and blow-dryer and got it
into some sort of order, but a restless night aboard the jet
had done it no good at all. Nevertheless, it had done the job
it was intended to do: it had got me safely past the watchers
at the gatehouse.

'Oh, that!' I gave a light laugh. If not satisfied, Madame
looked quite capable of bringing in the police to question
me. 'I decided on this trip on the spur of the moment. I
hadn't time to get to the hairdresser, so I wore a wig to
travel in.' I reached up and pulled it off, shaking my own
hair free.

'Ah, oui!' Madame said flatly. Her expression told me that
there was not much to choose between the wig and the
natural hair.

'Perhaps,' I placated, 'Madame might be kind enough to
recommend a hairdresser in Brussels to me?'

'Of course, of course.' Madame was instantly mollified
by this appeal; she would undoubtedly get a commission on
any customers she sent to local businesses. 'We have excellent hairdressers here. So sensible of you, Miss Bradstone,
to wait until your arrival to have your hair done. I will give
you address of my own hairdresser.' She tore the top sheet
from a notepad and scribbled rapidly.

While she did so, I unzipped my holdall and hurriedly
stuffed the wig inside. I would take it out in my room and
try to restore it; I would need it on the way back.

'That is all your baggage?' It had been an unwise move to draw Madame's attention to that. Again, suspicion radiated from those cold eyes.

'I was planning to do a lot of shopping here. I've heard you have so many lovely things. Perhaps Madame would be so kind as to advise me of the best bargains . . .?'

'Ah, oui!' It worked again. Madame's eyes softened at the thought of the commissions to be received from the establishments she recommended.

'Brussels lace!' she said decisively. 'And our chocolates —the finest in the world. And the fashions—ah, the fashions! In the arcades—I will give you the addresses. And you must tell them that I sent you, so that they will give you the discount.' She returned my passport, now far more interested in the possibilities unfolding before her. She began scribbling on the notepad again.

'You're very kind,' I said, 'but there's no hurry for that. I'd like to go to my room and rest for a while first. The flight was very tiring . . .'

'Of course, of course.' Madame turned and removed a key from a nest of numbered pigeonholes behind her. 'You have number thirty-three, very nice. On the third floor. The ascenseur is over there. I will have the shops and addresses waiting for you when you have rested.'

'Thank you.' I took the key and retreated in the direction she pointed. It was one of the doors I had assumed led into another room; now I noticed the discreet arrowed button beside it. I opened the door and hesitated, but Madame had returned to her notes, making it clear that I was to find my way to my room by myself.

Actually, it was just as well. There was not really room for Madame in the miniature elevator. Any two people travelling up or down in it together would have to be very good friends.

Or honeymooners. Tad and Inga, crowding into it with their luggage, must have laughed and enjoyed the slow ascent. For a moment, I could picture them and be glad for the happiness Tad had found. The life he had led from the time of his desertion to his marriage could not have been easy. Buck had done nothing to help him—on the contrary. It was not until after the Amnesty for Vietnam deserters that Tad had been able to draw on his inheritance from our parents. Buck could not stop him then, but Buck had been willing to grant no private amnesty. His trust betrayed had been more important to him than any betrayal of a country subsequently prepared to forgive that betrayal. Buck would never forgive. I could only be grateful that he was not prepared to vent his hostility on the next generation.

The elevator creaked upwards and I realized that there was no inner door. I pressed against the back as the floors slid past. It was a common European design, I knew, but it still did not seem safe to me. Not when any momentary carelessness could have such dire consequences.

I fought down a sense of panic as we passed the third floor and the elevator continued to rise. Then I remembered that the floors would be numbered in the European manner, our second floor being counted as their first, so that I would actually be one floor higher than I had expected.

The elevator juddered to a halt as it drew even with the next floor level and I wasted no time in flinging open the door and hurling myself into the dimly-lit corridor. The door to the elevator closed behind me and then there was no light at all.

Instinctively, I stretched out a hand to find the wall and recoiled as it brushed against something soft and furry. It was only the wallpaper, I reassured myself, I had noticed the fuzzy heavily-flocked wallpaper downstairs. It was not some high-climbing mouse, furry bug, nor even a patch of mould.

Bracing myself, I stretched out my hand again, a little lower this time. There should be a time-switch somewhere . . .

Ah, there it was. A dim bulb glowed overhead, not shedding as much radiance as the reflected light from the *ascenseur*. But enough to let me move along the corridor and find room No. 33 before there was a sharp click and darkness fell again. They didn't give you much time here. I wished I had thought to pack a pencil flashlight, it would help in finding the keyhole.

I poked around in what I deemed the general vicinity and, finally, the key slid into the lock. I twisted it rather frantically and pushed hard. The door swung inwards abruptly and I fell into the room, the door slammed behind me.

So this was a 'family accommodation'. Two single beds and a child's cot, an armchair, a dressing-table and the ubiquitous television set. There were two other doors; one led into a closet with not quite enough coathangers for an average family on holiday; the other, thank heavens, led into a bathroom. I would not have to face the dark corridor unless I was on my way in or out—and I was not going to stay here long enough to worry about it.

At least the room was bright and cheerful—although almost anything would have seemed so after that corridor. I crossed to the window and looked down on the street below. We were at the front of the house, high enough so that sunlight filtered into the room, in direct contrast to the gloomy street below. The high terraced buildings cut off most of the sun; even at noon, the street would seem dark. Perhaps it had been a bustle of activity earlier, with people on their way to work, but I doubted it. It seemed to be a quiet backwater where nothing ever happened—unless, perhaps, it was something sinister.

As I watched, a tall figure rounded the far corner and sauntered along the opposite side of the street, foreshortened and casting a long shadow. There was something vaguely familiar about him.

Tad! I had not realized I harboured such a ridiculous

hope until it sprang into my mind. Inga had managed to contact him, after all, and told him to meet us here! I took a deep breath and recognized the wildly optimistic idea as another variation of the wish-fulfilment daydream I had had in the first years of Tad's disgrace. In the dream, he would arrive home suddenly, in his uniform, covered with medals and explain that he had really been on a secret mission and it had been necessary for him to pretend that he had deserted in order to fool the enemy. But all the time he had really been a hero.

Children never give up. I hadn't thought there was that much childishness left in me.

In front of the hotel, the man paused and looked up. Now I could place him: the strange man who had caused such a commotion in the line at the check-in desk at Logan Airport. What was he doing at the *Poisson d'Or?*

I drew back from the window, although he couldn't possibly see me, squinting up, as he was, with the sun in his eyes. My nerves fluttered and I tried to assure myself that Brussels wasn't really that big. A tourist who wished to explore the old part of the town might easily stray along even this unpromising street, it was not all that far from the *Grand Place.* I was exhausted and jet-lagged; this was no time to let my nerves get the better of me.

When I peeped out of the window again, he was gone. At least, he was not directly outside the hotel. After a moment, I spotted him farther down the street, looking at the entrance of another building. Just a tourist hunting for a cheap hotel. Part of his trouble at the airport had concerned money, I remembered. I was glad he had decided against this place. As I watched, he moved again, crossed the street and disappeared from my line of vision.

I yawned and turned to consider the beds. They looked lumpy, but a judicious prodding of the nearest one revealed that the lumpiness was just the duvet and the mattress was quite adequate. I kicked off my shoes and sank down on it.

It was a nuisance that Inga was not here waiting for me, but there was nothing I could do about it. Just wait for her. I had not counted on wasting time like this.

I couldn't even sightsee—not that I was particularly interested. If I went out, I might miss her arrival. All I wanted was to get Jan-Carl and catch the next jet home.

The best thing I could do now was get some rest, so that I would be fresh and ready to move when Inga did show up.

The *Grand Place* was golden with the glow of discreetly placed spotlights, its ornate seventeenth-century Guild Houses looking like something out of a fairy tale. At pavement level, sidewalk cafés were crowded with festive customers enjoying the mild weather and strong drinks. I might have enjoyed some of it myself, if I had not been so annoyed. Enforced sightseeing is never so pleasant as the voluntary kind and I had no desire to see any sights at all. All I wanted was to collect Jan-Carl and go home, but I was stuck here overnight and all their quaintsy-cutesy mediæval square was not going to make me like it.

I had been roused from an uneasy sleep and even more uneasy dreams by an urgent summons to the telephone. Of course there was no telephone in the room, that would have been too simple. I had to pad down to the end of the corridor, the lights going out before I reached the telephone hanging on the wall at the far end. I found the dangling receiver by following the cord, then thumped at the wall beside the telephone in hopes of finding another time switch. No such luck. Madame was far too clever to place it where patrons could waste electricity by using it during phone calls. Presumably, if they wanted to dial out, her motto was, 'Let them use matches'. At least, it felt like matchsticks beneath my stocking feet.

'Yes?' I didn't bother to try to disguise my annoyance as I spoke into the mouthpiece. 'Who is it? What is it?' The

way things were going, I would not have been surprised to
find that it was Madame ringing up to tout some more shops
to me.

'Hope? Hope . . . it is you, yes?'

'Inga? Inga, where are you? I've been here for hours.
When are you arriving?'

'Oh, Hope, I am so sorry, but . . . It is not so easy.'

'What do you mean? Where are you?' My suspicions were
now fully roused. 'Are you even in Belgium? Don't tell me
you're not coming!'

'You do not understand. I cannot leave just yet. It . . . it
is not easy.'

'Inga, you've dragged me away from home at a time
when my grandfather is dying. You've booked me into this
wretched little hotel in a strange country where I don't
speak the language—and now you tell me it isn't easy for
*you!*'

'Hope, do not be angry. I try. I cannot be there tonight,
as I thought. You must wait. We are coming. There are
problems . . .'

'It isn't money, is it? Don't worry about that. I have
plenty with me. Just get here.'

'No, no, money is no problem. It is just . . . they are
watching us.'

'Who? Inga, who's watching you? Why should they? What
sort of trouble are you in? What's going on?'

'I will tell you tomorrow. Wait for us, please wait.' She
sounded close to tears. 'You must take Jan-Carl away with
you. Please.'

'All right.' I had no choice, really. I had come to get
Jan-Carl, I could not leave without him. 'Tomorrow. As
early as you can make it. I don't want to hang around here
any longer than I have to.'

'Yes, early, yes. Until tomorrow.' She had hung up before
I could say another word.

In the sudden silence, I felt that someone was watching

me, as well. I whirled around and wondered if I really had heard a door close softly as I did so.

As I made my way back to my room, my eyes slightly adjusted to the darkness, I realized how stupid I had been. I had stood in an open corridor, babbling about having plenty of money with me. It would be my own fault if I were robbed. I would never have made such a rudimentary mistake at home. I could only hope that no one had heard me. It would not be practicable to put my money into the hotel safe—even presuming that this place had such a thing —when I might need to move swiftly at any moment.

Well, not until morning now, but that was precious little comfort. I might just as well go out and spend a bit of that money now. I was hungry and I might even pick up a couple of souvenirs. Perhaps some chocolates for Ada and something to amuse Buck . . .

So, here I was in the *Grand Place*, wandering around the perimeter of the Square, reading the menus posted outside the restaurants and cafés, trying to decide what I felt like eating. Some of the smells wafting out from the doorways were delicious, but I wished I had paid better attention during French lessons in school. Some of it was familiar, but there were quite a few words I could not translate at all.

'You got to be careful,' a doom-laden voice spoke behind me. 'They eat horsemeat around here.'

'What?' Startled, I whirled to face the woman who had been behind me in the check-in line at Logan Airport.

'It says so right here in my guidebook,' she assured me. 'They think it's a great delicacy. Europe! I don't know why my daughter wants to live over here. They're all crazy!'

There was no answer to that. I stared at her, telling myself that the *Grand Place* in Brussels was like those various hotels in unlikely places where, sooner or later, everyone in the world was supposed to pass by. Especially if they had arrived on the same plane and were sightseeing.

'Say—' The woman seemed to be following the same train of thought. 'You were on my plane, weren't you? You've done something with your hair since you got here —it looks a lot better.'

'Oh, yes—I *did* see you on the plane.' That was as much as I was prepared to admit. I was certainly not going to get into a dialogue about my hair. 'Did you have a pleasant flight? I wasn't able to sleep very well, were you?'

'I never sleep on a plane. I hate them.'

'Perhaps you should have come by ship.'

'I hate them, too. I hate being here. But I gotta see my daughter every once in a while and make sure she's really okay. You can't tell from letters. I got another daughter married in the States, like a sensible person, and I don't hafta worry about her—well, not very much. Anyhow, I also like to see my little European grandchildren, even though it kills me to hear them talking a foreign language instead of American like they ought to.'

'Yes, well, I'm sure they'll speak English when they're a bit older.'

'Oh, they speak it now, but it ain't the same.'

That was probably all to the good. I didn't say it. I gave her a feeble smile and moved along. To my dismay, she fell into step beside me. It seemed that having been on the same plane was as good as a proper introduction by a mutual friend. It was all we needed for an instant comradeship.

'I'm ready for something else to eat, too,' she confided. 'I had a couple of them waffles a while ago, but they don't stand by you. Just like Chinese food, you get hungry again in no time.'

I smiled weakly, recognizing that I was trapped. Short of cutting and running, which would make me look ridiculous, there was no way of escaping her. On the other hand, why not act like a normal tourist for tonight? She wouldn't be my first choice for a companion, but most people travelling alone linked up with chance-met acquaintances for a meal or excursion. She wasn't so appalling that she could ruin my appetite and having someone else to talk to—or, rather, listen to—might keep my mind off my own problems. I had to eat something and I felt awkward about going into a strange restaurant on my own. I was not the assured world traveller I would like to have been. Buck's increasing frailty over these past years had curtailed or postponed many of the trips I might have taken.

'I'm Irma Danziger,' she offered—and waited expectantly.

'Oh . . . yes. I . . .' Suddenly, I felt that I did not want her to know my real name. 'I'm Hope Bradley.'

'Pleased to meet you,' she said solemnly.

I wondered whether her etiquette demanded the response that the pleasure was all mine, but I refused to perjure myself to that extent.

'I'm glad I ran into you,' she said. 'To tell the truth, I was beginning to feel kinda lost all by myself.'

'Then you're not meeting your daughter here?'

'No, she don't live right in Belgium. Maybe my son-in-law will come to collect me. I ain't heard nothing from them yet. I'll just hafta hang around. Sooner or later, somebody's bound to show up.'

It sounded as though we were in the same boat. I hoped I could rely on Inga's promise that she would be here in the morning, but I was already beginning to realize that my sister-in-law's assurances were not based on solid fact. More worryingly, her insistence on some mysterious *They* was raising the suspicion in my mind that she might be slightly paranoid. Or more than slightly.

All the more reason to get Jan-Carl away from her and back to the States and the safety and stability of a proper family life.

Lost in my thoughts, I barely noticed that we had turned a couple of corners, leaving the brightly-lit tourist sector, and were heading down a dark winding street. It might be another residential district; the houses had wooden inner shutters fastened across windows to shut in the light and warmth and close out the rest of the world. It was the sort of place where you could scream and scream, with no one to hear you—or bother to investigate if they did.

'Irma—' I glanced uneasily at my companion—'do you know where we're going?'

'Going?' Her face was shadowed, but she sounded surprised by my question. 'I thought we were looking for a restaurant.'

'There doesn't seem to be any along here. I think we should turn back to the *Grand Place*.'

'I'm pretty sure I can see one just ahead.' She kept moving. 'It's in a basement. Down some steps.'

'I don't think so.' I halted. 'It's all dark ahead. Let's go back.'

'Are you calling me a liar?' She whirled on me, suddenly belligerent.

'No, I just think you're mistaken.' I began backing away from her. Never mind Inga's paranoia, it began to seem more than possible that I had landed myself with a mental case here and now. And idiotically walked off into the darkness with her.

'There's one on this street. I know it. Come on!'

'No. Let's try another street.' I backed farther away as she showed signs of being about to grab my arm and try to drag me with her. If I could just get a bit more distance between us, I would turn and run—and to hell with looking ridiculous!

'Oh!' I had backed into a solid presence. I tried to sidestep it, but it blocked me.

'Well, well, well,' a male voice said. 'Look who's here!'

# CHAPTER 5

'Who's there?' Irma advanced, peering into the gloom.

'You mean, as in Friend or Foe? Or do you want my name, rank and serial number? They won't mean a thing to you, anyway, we've never been introduced.'

He spoke English and he was a third person, his presence suspending the uneasy duel we had been waging. I was prepared to greet him as a friend.

'Don't be so fresh.' Already, Irma was sounding better—annoyed, but normal. 'Who are you?'

'We're lost,' I said quickly. 'Whoever you are, could you please direct us back to the *Grand Place*?'

'I'll do better than that,' he said. 'I'll escort you personally.'

'You don't need to bother. We're doing all right.'

'Thank you.' I took his arm firmly, before he could get away. 'I'd appreciate that. We were really lost.'

'Didn't your mothers ever warn you about roaming around strange cities after dark all by yourselves?'

He seemed to know where he was going. We turned another corner and the streetlights became brighter. There was music somewhere in the distance.

'We thought we knew where we were going.' I was feeling more cheerful with every step we took. 'But we must have taken a wrong turning. We were looking for a restaurant.'

'Any particular one? Your guidebook should have given you clearer directions. Not that you could read them where you were.'

There would be no trouble reading anything now. We were approaching the *Grand Place*. Irma and I had not wandered so far, after all. It was a little disturbing to realize just how swiftly a wrong turn or two could carry the unwary tourist deep into the heart of unknown territory. I remembered the newspaper reports a few years ago about the finding of a woman's skeleton in an Egyptian tomb—another tourist who had taken a couple of wrong turnings. And never found her way back.

I shivered involuntarily and moved more quickly towards the bright lights and the promise of warmth and people. Lots of people. Nothing could happen in front of so many witnesses.

'Cold?' My rescuer looked down at me in some concern. 'What you need is a drink.'

'That sounds pretty good to me.' Irma perked up. 'The sooner, the better. My feet are killing me.'

If she insisted on wearing shoes like that, it was not surprising. Black patent leather high heels were not the ideal footwear for cobblestoned streets. It was a wonder she hadn't turned her ankle. My natural optimism returning, it occurred to me that she might yet.

'Perhaps you'd like to go back to your hotel and rest.' My rescuer was an optimist, too. 'It was a very tiring trip.'

'I ain't that tired!' As we stepped into the brightness of the lights of a corner sidewalk café, she turned to glare at him and her face changed. 'Hot damn—it's him again!'

She was right. I had last seen him meandering down the street outside my hotel. Before that, he had been in the line at the Reservations Desk at Logan. Was the world really *that* small?

'Well,' I said, somewhat caustically, 'this is getting to be quite a gathering of the clans—the Bostonian Clan, that is.'

'We ought to stick together,' he said, looking at me. '"Strangers in a strange land" and all that.'

'Yeah? Well, let me tell you: you're too strange for me! Come on!' Irma grabbed my arm and tugged at it. 'Let's get away from this creep. I already had trouble with him at the airport.'

'No, don't go.' He had my other arm and was holding me

where I was. 'You were mistaken about me. I can explain.'

Between the two of them, I was going to be black-and-blue in the morning. In fact, I would be lucky if they didn't dislocate an arm.

'Come and have a drink,' he urged. 'Let's talk this over.'

'Don't go with him.' Irma tugged at my arm again. 'He's only after your money.'

'Has she got any?' His face brightened.

'Anybody's got more than you have!'

'True, unfortunately,' he sighed. 'Only too true.'

'See—' she said to me. 'Let's go!'

'However—' He retained his grip on my arm. 'My credit card is still in good working order and I would be delighted if you ladies would join me for dinner. I hate to eat alone.'

'Oh,' Irma said. 'Well, maybe that's different. You're sure—' she looked at him suspiciously—'your credit card hasn't expired, or something?'

'Positive. And my credit is still good—if that is what you were so delicately suggesting.'

'Look.' I pulled free of both of them. 'The only thing in danger of expiring around here is me, if I don't get some food soon.' Delicious smells were assailing me from all sides. 'Why don't we just split up and go our own ways?'

'No, no. We've only just met—'

'You don't wanna be alone on your first night in Europe. I don't, either.'

I tried to remember the last time I had experienced such a passion for my company. I think it was at school on the days when my allowance arrived.

'We might as well stick together—at least for the course of a meal. I insist, I'm paying.'

'He's right.' Irma called a truce. 'It's a time we ate. I'm starving.'

'So am I.' He repossessed my arm. 'I'm so hungry I could eat a horse.'

'You're probably going to.' Irma took my other arm and I was back in the middle, neatly captured again. 'Didn't you read your guidebook yet?'

'I haven't had time. That place over there looks good.'

'Fine.' I was glad that he had opted for a restaurant right on the *Grand Place*. I had had enough of dark winding streets.

'Suits me.'

We found an outside table and seated ourselves. A waiter rushed over and distributed menus. There was a blissful silence as we studied them. I wondered how well Irma was doing with hers; somehow, I did not think she was much of a linguist.

'The *Moules Marinières* are very good here,' our host announced.

'I don't like mussels any better than I like horses.' Irma glared at him. 'Don't these foreigners ever eat anything decent?'

'You could always have the chicken,' I suggested. 'That's usually safe.'

'I suppose.' She continued to scan the menu gloomily. 'My son-in-law took me to a place in Paris once, they had pigs' snouts on the menu. I was almost sick when I saw it. I swear he done it on purpose.'

We all shuddered companionably, although I suspected that our host's shudder arose more from visualizing Irma as a mother-in-law than from any thought of bizarre menu items.

'By the way—' That reminded me. 'Shouldn't we introduce ourselves? This is Irma Danziger, I'm Hope Brad . . . ley. And you are—?'

'Russ. Russell . . . Adamson.' Had he hesitated over his name? 'And I'm going to have *steak au poivre* and *Stella Artois* —beer to you.'

'And horsemeat to you, I'm sure. I wouldn't trust that for a minute. I guess I *will* have the chicken.'

'So will I.' It was easier than making a decision of my own. 'But I'd prefer wine, please.'

'I guess I'll stick with the beer. I'll be drinking enough wine when my son-in-law orders the meals.'

Russ gestured to the hovering waiter and gave our orders. There was some discussion about the wine, but I let them argue it out. Some of the lights around us seemed to have dimmed. The network of little streets radiating out from the square was no longer so clearly defined. It was growing late and even the most determined tourist traps were closing down for the night.

Above us, the great mediæval buildings loomed, the subdued floodlighting both illuminating and shadowing the windows and turrets, the balconies, statues and *bas-reliefs*. They were imposing and somehow frightening. They had been here for centuries; they would outlast us all. We could sit in their shadow and wine and dine, but then we would go away and live out our little lives and die. They would endure. I felt suddenly as though I were being crushed by the weight of history.

*Buck . . .* Buck was in the process of passing into history. He had lived and flourished, built his business empire throughout most of the twentieth century and made his name famous; but he was only human, not bricks and mortar. Soon he would be nothing but an entry in the history books yet to be written; a couple of pages in some, a footnote in others. Buck would have hated being a footnote.

'What's the matter? You ain't feeling sick, are you? Before you eat anything at all?'

'No, I—I'm all right. Just tired, thank you.'

'I hope that's all. You don't want to get sick in a foreign country. Maybe you should move to my hotel and I can keep an eye on you.'

'I'll be all right. Some food will help.'

'It should be here soon.' Russ cocked a wary eye at me.

'Not a touch of tourist tummy, is it? You were looking decidedly pensive.'

'More like tourist imagination.' I took refuge in a half-truth. 'All this history suddenly got on top of me. These buildings . . . they've seen so much, lasted so long. While we . . .'

'*Out, brief candle!*' He knew what I meant. Or almost. He hadn't known Buck, who had shone so brilliantly and was now guttering towards extinction, leaving us all in darkness.

'Where are the candles?' We had lost Irma—would that we could physically, as well. 'Are we supposed to have one at our table? That restaurant next door has them on every table.'

The food arrived, saving us from further explanation. I had the feeling that Irma would rate Shakespeare somewhere above the horsemeat and below the *moules*.

'What's this yellow stuff beside the French Fries?' She had found a fresh grievance on her plate.

'It's mayonnaise,' Russ said. 'That's the way they serve them in Belgium. In England, they put vinegar on them.'

'You're kidding me.' She poked a fork cautiously into the yellow mass and tasted it gingerly. 'It *is* mayonnaise!'

'Would I lie to you?'

'You would, if you could. Boy, am I gonna be glad to get back to the States. The things your family put you through!'

There was a thoughtful silence. I tried not to think about my family again. I was doing everything that I could do, but already this trip had taken longer than I expected. Before we flew back tomorrow, I must try to telephone home and see how Buck was doing. '*Hurry* . . .' he had said.

'You don't have to eat it, if you don't want to,' Russ said.

'Oh, I'm sorry.' I stabbed blindly at my chicken. 'I'm afraid I was lost in thought.'

'History doesn't seem to have a very good effect on you. Tomorrow, I'd recommend that you take a look at modern Belgium. It's completely up-to-date, you know. Give the museums a miss until your culture shock recedes. Stroll around and see the Atomium, and the EEC Buildings, visit some shops . . .'

'You sound like my hotel proprietor. She's mad keen to get me into the shops, too. I think she gets a commission.'

'Why don't we go shopping tomorrow?' Irma took up the idea eagerly. 'I'm gonna hafta bring back souvenirs for everybody at home, aren't you? We can get that outa the way, then do some more sightseeing.'

'I can't!' I blurted it out with unflattering haste. Her eyes narrowed. 'I mean, I'm meeting someone—some friends— in the morning. We have other plans.'

'It was just a thought.' She jabbed her fork into a large *frite*, gathered a dollop of mayonnaise on it and absently ate it. 'I don't suppose we could join up, just the same?'

'I'm sorry, it's quite impossible.' I hurriedly crammed some chicken into my own mouth to cut off the need for further explanations. It was none of her business, anyway. Just because we had travelled on the same plane, it didn't entitle her to spend the rest of her tour with me. And why should she want to? For all she knew, I had spent all my money on my plane ticket—or had she seen how much I had left over?

Several more lights were dimmed around us and dishes began rattling suggestively in the background. The table beside us had emptied long ago, now a waiter whisked away the tablecloth and began upending the chairs on to the bare table.

'I think they're trying to tell us something,' I said thank-fully. I was more than ready to receive the message. It had been a long day, but the prospect of escaping from my companions was revivifying me.

'I thought things stayed open later here,' Irma grumbled.

Chimes rang out from a nearby clock tower. It was later than we had thought.

'I'll walk you to your hotels,' Russ said.

'Don't bother. We can find our way back.'

I wasn't so sure of that—nor did I like that *we*. There seemed to be a dearth of taxis here in the old town and I had no confidence in Irma's talent as a navigator. We had already been badly lost once this evening.

'Thank you,' I said. At least I knew he knew where my hotel was; I had seen him exploring that street earlier in the day.

'You're not going to let him?' Irma stared at me in horror. 'You don't know where you'd end up.'

*With your throat cut, in a dark alley,* her tone implied. I was suddenly conscious that I was carrying an inordinate amount of cash and had never seen either of these people before yesterday.

'Look,' he said to Irma. 'I'll tell you what we'll do. We'll *both* walk Hope home and then—'

'And then nothing! I ain't walking off into the wild blue yonder alone with you, Buster! No way!'

She might wait until she'd been invited. I concentrated on the last inch or so of wine in my glass and avoided looking at either of them.

'What a shame. I was so looking forward to showing you the *Manneken Pis* by moonlight.'

'I bet you were! You got a filthy mind!' She turned to me. 'I don't think we should let him take us nowhere. I don't trust him.'

The waiter arrived with our bill and I noticed that she trusted him to pay it. I smothered a yawn.

'Okay, if you feel that way,' she said. 'We'll both walk you back to your hotel. Then I'm ditching him. I can get back to my hotel alone. I ain't afraid of no muggers.'

'*Au contraire,*' Russ murmured. 'As the Frenchman said when he was asked if he had dined aboard the Channel ferry.'

'Look.' She ignored him elaborately. 'Why don't we meet for breakfast tomorrow? Before your friends arrive.'

'Why don't we all meet for breakfast?' Russ amended.

There I was again, the most popular girl in the class. They couldn't bear to be parted from me—even at the price of putting up with each other. It was making me very uneasy.

Had I displayed too much of my money at the airport? Were they really partners in some kind of elaborate confidence game? If so, they were doomed to failure. They certainly hadn't inspired any confidence in me. *Au contraire,* as Russ had said.

'We'll be having breakfast in our own hotels.' I aimed a low blow at the spot where Irma would feel it most—her pocketbook. 'It's paid for—breakfast comes with the room, remember?'

'Oh, yeah.' She was momentarily nonplussed. 'That's right.'

Before she could recover, I pushed back my chair. They all had to stand then. We were on our way.

'Don't worry.' Russ tapped her lightly on the shoulder. 'It's a small world. We're sure to see each other again.'

Not, I decided, if I saw them first.


## CHAPTER 6

Despite my exhaustion, I slept badly—and infrequently. Worse than on the plane. My catnaps were haunted by nightmares, so that I was relieved as each one broke off abruptly, hurtling me back to wakefulness. Distant church chimes marked every hour and quarter-hour. The wind was rising and, somewhere before dawn, rain began slashing at the windows.

It was going to be a nice day for a funeral. I heard myself moaning as I slid back into a nightmare. Buck was there—but they weren't burying him. He was still strong and vigorous. Not young—I had never known him young. Ada was almost young; they were laughing together at something she had just said, something I could not quite hear.

And Tad—Tad was there, in his uniform. He snapped to attention, saluting Buck. They all laughed again. There wasn't a cloud in the sky, no shadows over the scene. That was odd; there weren't even shadows where there should be. No one was casting a shadow. I was there, and yet I wasn't. But I had no shadow, either.

Aunt Florence came out of the house and said something to them. There were shadows then—on their faces. Buck sighed and gave his arm to Ada, Tad fell in behind them. The front door opened and a procession marched slowly out carrying a wreath-laden coffin. I knew what was wrong then. They weren't ghosts—I was.

*They were burying me . . .*

I wrenched myself awake and threw back the duvet. It was still raining, but light enough in the room to read my watch. Daylight, such as it was, had dawned at last. I could give up the struggle of trying to sleep.

And it was still a nice day for a funeral. I shivered and got out of bed. Nothing at all would be gained if I allowed myself to give way to depression. It would be self-indulgent to sit on the side of the bed and break into tears. Buck had trained me better than that.

Buck had trained Tad, too. Or thought he had . . . *And stop that this minute!* The past can't be changed; brooding does no good.

The shower was brutally cold. Even when I forgave myself and turned on the hot tap, there was little improvement. At least it jolted me fully awake and drove away the demons.

I dressed and went downstairs to the residents' dining-room for coffee and croissants with sweet unsalted butter and black cherry jam.

'*Guten Morgen.*' Two of my fellow guests greeted me as

they went past, handbags swinging, to what was apparently their usual table by the window.

At another table, a pair of husky youths discussed the day's agenda in voices that sounded almost American, except that their r's were too pronounced. Rucksacks at their feet were decorated with Canadian maple leaf badges.

A bearded professor-type sat alone and never raised his eyes from his book, not even when he poured more coffee into his cup. Long practice had obviously made him an expert at it.

Other tables bore the debris of demolished *petits déjeuners*. It seemed we were the late breakfast brigade. People with work to do were already on their way to that work. Or perhaps they just had serious tourist schedules.

I wouldn't mind having some proper work to do myself. At home, at this hour, I would be well into my morning's work, acting as Buck's secretary; a job which had been given to me so that I could learn the inner workings of Bradstone Enterprises, with a view to my eventual inheritance. My Cousin Everett would have left for the Boston Office, where he was already entrenched as Vice-Chairman.

Here, I tried to refill my cup, but the tiny coffee-pot only relinquished half a cup more before the stream from its nozzle dwindled to a trickle and stopped. Not much coffee to linger over.

It began to dawn on me that it was not going to be easy to hang around here killing time while I waited for Inga to appear. Already, Madame was clearing the vacant tables, her smile a little too bright, her manner a little too pointed. Everyone connected with the catering trade was an expert at moving reluctant customers away from their tables.

The professor absently drained the last of his coffee, threw down his napkin, pushed back his chair and ambled from the room, all without raising his eyes from his book. He cleared the door-jamb with half an inch to spare and vanished from my sight.

I turned to the window. It was still raining. My gaze crossed those of the German women and they nodded cordially and smiled. It would be easy to strike up a conversation —too easy.

'A bad day,' one of them said. 'It will not spoil your sightseeing, I hope?'

For an instant, I thought she knew my name, then realized what she had actually said. In English. Was my nationality so obvious?

'Perhaps it will stop before long,' I said. 'I'll wait a while and see.'

The Canadian students looked up at the burst of English conversation, then returned to their map. The German women were too old to be of interest—and they certainly had no time for someone so unadventurous that she was going to let a little rain change her plans.

'You could have your hair done this morning.' Madame frowned at me, already suspecting that I was not going to go out spending all that money, a portion of which she had earmarked for herself.

'In this rain?' The other German woman entered the lists on my side. 'A hairdo would be destroyed before she returned here.'

'She could buy an umbrella!' Madame snapped. 'She could go to the Gallery St Caubert. There are many beautiful shops there—and it is all under cover.'

In short, she'd rather have me do anything except hang around here. Which was just too bad, as hanging around here was my only plan for the day and Madame was just going to have to lump it.

'She could also visit the Ilot Sacré district,' the first German woman suggested. 'There are many arcades there.'

The Canadians downed their maps and swilled the last of their coffee. Such woman-talk was boring them. They shouldered their backpacks, said goodbye to Madame, nodded to us and left.

Madame swooped to clear their table. There was a finality in the way she clattered the dishes.

Even the German women recognized it. They rose and left. I could linger no longer. At least, not in the dining-room.

'Is there a residents' lounge?' I braved Madame's fury again. 'I really ought to write some postcards before I do anything else.'

'Do you have any postcards?'

'Er, no. I thought perhaps—'

'I can sell you some! They are at the desk.' She shepherded me out into the reception area and stood over me as I selected far too many postcards, which I had no intention of sending. I would be home before any postcards could reach there.

'The lounge is on the next floor,' she informed me, as she took some American dollars and returned Belgian francs in change. I had the feeling that she had gained on the exchange. She was more cheerful. 'At the front. Very nice. You can see when the rain stops.' She was still determined to get rid of me.

The lounge was bleak and cheerless. There was a small fireplace, but a vase of artificial flowers stood in the grate in warning to anyone who expected a fire instead. The windows had apparently been hermetically sealed against the impending winter—from the dusty, musty smell of the room, they might never have been opened.

The only thing the lounge had going for it was the discarded English language newspaper I found on a table in the corner. I wondered if it had belonged to the Professor. It was a couple of days old, but the headlines were all new to me. They shrieked of FRAUD IN COMMON MARKET ... BUTTER MOUNTAINS ... WINE LAKES ... FARMERS IN UPROAR ... GREEN POUND ... LORRIES INTERCEPTED ... LAMB CARCASES SPRAYED WITH PAINT ... EURO MPs IN PROTEST ...

All the fun of the fair. It meant little or nothing to me. I leafed through it idly, prepared to drop it and be discovered busily writing my postcards if Madame decided to check up on me. I also remained close to the window so that I could watch the street below. Inga and Jan-Carl should be arriving at any time now.

By the time I had read through the paper for a second time, discovering only that crime lurked in the unlikeliest corners and the entire Common Market seemed at the mercy of fraudulent operators, I began to wonder if Inga was going to stand me up again. It was now well into the morning, the rain was slackening and the sky was beginning to lighten. The angry drone of a vacuum cleaner had been drawing closer in the corridor outside. I had the fated feeling that it would not be long before Madame appeared in the doorway to drive me out into what was left of the storm so that she could have her domain to herself for a few hours.

I hurriedly tossed the newspaper aside, reached for a postcard and became very busy scribbling nonsense across its blank space. The vacuum cleaner thumped against the lounge door. I braced myself for the invasion; then, in the distance, a telephone rang.

With a final bad-tempered thump, the vacuum cleaner cut out and a moment later, the telephone stopped ringing. Unfortunately, I had only a few moments to enjoy the silence.

There was a sharp vindictive rap on the door; it swung open triumphantly. 'The telephone, it is for you,' the maid said.

I might have known it. With a conciliatory smile, I went down the hallway. The telephone was in roughly the same position it occupied on the upper floor. The only difference was that there was a window near this one.

'Hope? Hope, it is Inga. Now, Hope, you must be calm.'

'Why?' I could hear my voice rising. There are few more ominous openings to a conversation than to be told you must keep calm. 'Why must I be calm, Inga? What is it *now?*' A sudden suspicion assailed me. 'Where *are* you? You're not in Brussels, are you?'

'We are in Cologne. We cannot come to Brussels. But it is all right. You must meet us in Luxembourg instead.'

'Luxembourg?' I took a deep breath and lowered my voice. 'It may be all right with you, Inga, but it isn't all right with me. I'm not even sure where Luxembourg *is*. What's wrong with Brussels?'

'It is not safe in Brussels. They are watching. Perhaps they are already waiting there.'

'Inga—' I resolved that I was going to get that woman into the hands of a good psychiatrist as soon as possible. 'Inga, what *They?* Who are you hiding from? And why?'

'There is good train service to Luxembourg,' Inga went on implacably. 'You get on the train at Brussels Nord or Brussels Midi and you get out at Luxembourg. There will be no problem.'

'Inga—'

'You leave the hotel now and get the next train. We will do the same. We will be waiting at Luxembourg.'

'Inga, this is ridiculous. You told me you'd be waiting in Brussels. I can't go chasing about all over Europe. I have to get home. Buck is . . . terminally ill.' I could not bring myself to say *dying*. Shadows from my nightmare still haunted me. Buck had seemed so strong, so alive . . .

'Jan-Carl is longing to meet you.' Inga played her trump card, reminding me of why I was here. 'He has heard so much about his aunt. He can hardly wait.'

'Inga—' I made one final effort. 'Please, Inga, bring him to Brussels. I'll meet you at the station, if you like, and we can go straight to the airport from there.'

'You do not understand,' she said stubbornly. 'Jan-Carl, he will be safer with you than with me. I see you soon.'

The line went dead.

Another delay. I replaced the receiver furiously. I would have to telephone home and let Ada know, but I could not telephone from here. Down the hallway, the vacuum cleaner was droning again, reminding me that there were listening ears—and practically everyone in the hotel spoke English. Perhaps that was why Tad had liked it.

The station. All railway stations had telephones and I could ring from there. No one would pay any attention to anything I might say. If only because there would be a higher proportion of non-English speaking people around.

I would get my holdall and leave now. If I connected with a train, I would make the call from Luxembourg. Otherwise, it would help to kill time until the next train left.

I went up to my room, abandoning the postcards on the table in the lounge, already thinking of the immediate problem my hasty departure would bring.

Madame was not going to like it.


## CHAPTER 7

It had been worthwhile staking out the hotel. The Bradstone Heiress was definitely up to something. Furthermore, he was not the only one interested in whatever it might be.

Not just the tiresome woman who had stuck like a burr last night, either. No, there were fresh members of the cast today—and all of them taking the same inordinate interest in the heiress. Why?

He leaned back against the wall of his vantage-point—a shadowed doorway of an empty building—and watched the traffic at the very busy entrance of the *Poisson d'Or*. If it were any busier, there would be a traffic jam.

Two backpackers had been the first to emerge. And then, oddly, had got no farther than the corner of the next street, where they halted and brought out a map. They had been puzzling over it ever since. If genuine, they must be the most inept hikers ever to attempt a European Tour. There was enough about the muscling of their exposed calves and their facial structure—not to mention the constant anxious glances back towards the entrance of the *Poisson d'Or*— to give rise to the suspicion that they were an extremely purposeful pair, carrying out other work under the guise of innocent hikers.

After them, at a respectable interval, had ambled a tall, bearded gentleman absorbed in a book which he, literally, had not been able to put down. Nor was he able to raise his eyes from it. So intent was he that he paused several steps from the entrance of the hotel and went into a trance over his reading matter. Only occasionally did his eyes flick upwards from the book to take in the hotel doorway.

*Very* interesting. Russ resisted a double temptation: on the one hand, to go up and tap the hikers on the shoulder and offer assistance in sending them in the right direction; on the other hand, to ask the scholar what was so profoundly absorbing. The world had a right to know the hitherto undiscovered masterpiece that could stop a man in his tracks until he had finished it.

Madame had appeared on the doorstep several times, looking to the left and to the right, yet giving no sign of recognizing her guests. Invariably, she had glanced sky-wards, as though checking the weather, then retreated into her domain again. He was left with the impression that, given world enough and time, Madame would bear further investigation.

Meanwhile, the vultures waited. Whatever they had in mind, the pickings would be good. He whiled the time away with some mental arithmetic. That mansion on the North Shore alone must be worth a few millions now—and add in a few more millions for all the land surrounding it. Then, the old boy had had a finger in most of the multinational pies since the late 1920s. He'd got in on the ground floor of some of the most spectacular of them.

The old boy had switched his buccaneering raids farther afield as war clouds gathered on the European horizon. He became a regular commuter on the old ocean liners and there were whispers that he had occasionally snatched a human brand from the burning in the course of the shrewd business deals he had pulled off in the track of the advancing armies.

He was too old for active service when Pearl Harbor had plunged his own nation into the war, but had become one of the first of Roosevelt's patriotic Dollar-a-Year men. That hadn't done him any financial harm, either. All those Washington contacts had given him a flying start in the postwar world, as the swords were being turned back into ploughshares.

Perhaps he had envisaged his grandson setting up his own Far Eastern network in the lulls between battles. He had been fast enough to push the kid into the Army. What he couldn't have foreseen was the effect it would have on the boy. Like so many others, Buck had not realized that the last of the clean and decent wars had been fought. Now they were dirty and drawn-out, no clear-cut victories, no stable loyalties, no big Welcome Home parades for the boys who came back. Too bad no one in Government had been bright enough to profit from the French experience in that territory. They'd had a bellyful of it when it was called French Indo-China.

Across the street, the door opened. Everyone snapped to guarded attention, but it was another false alarm. Two women stalked out and, looking neither to the left nor to the right, marched purposefully down to a corner of the street where they hailed a passing taxi.

The hikers creased their map into a fresh fold with a faint air of desperation. The absorbed reader turned another page. Russ considered lighting one of his increasingly rare cigarettes, but decided against it; there was no point in drawing attention to himself if he had not already been noticed.

It was as well the rain was stopping. Loitering on street-corners became even more pointed in bad weather. If any of the locals looked out of their windows and saw the same people hanging about for too long, they would be fully justified in calling the police. Even the world's worst map-readers could not spend an entire morning poring over their puzzle. Sooner or later they would have to fold up the map, strike out in some direction and get lost. Nor could the most avid reader justify a couple of hours rooted to the same spot with his book.

Russ was a bit concerned about his own weak cover. While the *International Herald-Tribune* was an excellent news-paper, he had been perusing his copy long enough to have memorized it.

Fortunately, the others were too busy trying to maintain their own acts to see through his. Or, if they did, they weren't going to admit it; they were all people in glass houses.

Speaking of houses, there was activity again in the vicinity of the *Poisson d'Or*. A taxi drew up outside and, after a moment, the Bradstone Heiress emerged, looking as though she had had a sleepless night. Looking, also, as though a sleepless night was the least of her troubles.

She spoke a few words to the taxi-driver, got in, and they drove away.

As soon as the taxi had rounded the corner, the two hikers folded up their map and began jogging after it.

The unputdownable book abruptly became disposable as the bearded man suddenly took possession of a parked car and started it up.

Russ thriftily folded the *International Herald-Tribune* and stowed it in his back pocket; it might come in useful again. He set off at a jaunty pace, just short of jogging. There was no hope of keeping up with the taxi, but he didn't mind bringing up the rear of the parade, so long as he was able to cross the finishing line in good time.

Years in a country that had insisted every film must be dubbed into the local language had left him rather good at lip-reading. He had had a clear view of Hope Bradstone's mouth when she spoke to the taxi driver. If she wasn't going to the railway station, he would turn in his Press Card.

And there she was, bless her beautiful diction. At the ticket window, handing over her cash and enunciating 'Luxembourg' so clearly that it would be impossible to mistake it for Cologne, Ostende, Amsterdam, or any of the myriad destinations available from Brussels.

He watched as she accepted her ticket, put away her change, and crossed the concourse to the telephones. He checked one of the timetables posted nearby; plenty of time. Time enough to buy his own ticket and even get something to eat in the station cafeteria. Time enough, also, to saunter past the telephones and see if he could lipread a bit more information.

On the way, Russ passed the news-stand and saw, without surprise, that the book-lover from the *Poisson d'Or* was carefully scanning the racks of English-language paperbacks, obviously looking for another book that would hold his interest the way the last one had. It was sheer coincidence, of course, that he had merely to turn slightly in order to have a clear view of the telephones.

Nor did Russ reel back in amazement when he came across that familiar scene in European railway stations: two hikers kneeling together, earnestly repacking their backpacks. Even before he moved into position to see their faces, he would have taken a bet on them. There weren't all that many backpacks sporting the maple leaf at this time of the year; North American colleges had already gone back into session.

It was a disappointment to find the Bradstone Heiress huddled over the telephone, her lips so close to the receiver that they could barely be discerned, let alone read. A natural defence mechanism—or a bad connection? No matter, the result was the same. It would be a waste of time to hang around hoping for any crumbs—or syllables—to drop from that table. He would be better occupied in getting himself something that could pass as brunch. The coffee and croissant he had had at the crack of dawn had long since ceased to sustain him.

Tempting though they were, Russ walked past the places selling *biers* and spirits. He had never been able to adapt to the Continental custom of alcohol at any hour of the morning, he wasn't sure whether it was because of a latent Puritanism or a healthy respect for his liver.

The cafeteria was uncrowded and, although the heavier dishes already listed on the menu did not tempt him, a cheese omelette seemed a happy compromise between breakfast and lunch. And you couldn't go wrong with coffee and toast.

He waited for the omelette to be freshly cooked, then loaded his tray and turned to choose a table. Midway across the room, someone waved to him.

'*Hail, hail*—' he murmured under his breath—'*the gang's all here . . .*'

Forcing a smile, he took a tighter grip on his tray and headed in her direction.

## CHAPTER 8

'He's still alive, if that's what you mean.' Ada was ever one to call a spade a spade—when she wasn't calling it a bloody shovel. 'We expected you back by now. What's gone wrong?'

'Nothing . . . at least, nothing very much.' I had put

through a person-to-person collect call, so Ada already knew that I was not calling from any American airport. 'At least, I don't think so . . .

'Oh, Ada—' Hearing that dear familiar voice again, I suddenly felt about ten years old. I wanted to throw my arms around her, rest my head on her comforting shoulder and burst into tears. Instead, I tightened my grip on the telephone and took a deep breath. 'Ada, it's such a mess.'

'What does that mean?' She sounded as though she were taking a few deep breaths at her end. 'What's happened over there?'

'It's all right. I'm just being silly. Just because Inga wasn't able to bring Jan-Carl to Brussels. I've got to meet her in Luxembourg to collect him. It means another delay, that's all. I hope it will be all right.'

'It should be,' Ada said. 'The old goat is going to hang on until you get here if it kills him.' She heard herself and gave a harsh laugh. 'You needn't worry about that. You know he never ran out on an important deal in his life. This is giving him something to live for—something extra. He wants to see Jan-Carl.'

'He will, I promise.' Even as I said it, I wondered if I were telling the truth. 'I'm at the station in Brussels right now, the train leaves in just over an hour. Inga swore she'd be waiting for me in Luxembourg—' She had sworn she'd be waiting for me in Brussels, too.

'It's all right,' Ada said. 'We never really expected you to be back as fast as you thought you would. This time of year, you can get hurricane winds, fog, all sorts of delays . . .'

Of course, she had often travelled with Buck. I closed my eyes and could see her, as I'd seen her so many times, returning from a trip with Buck, swathed in a mink coat which had mysteriously disappeared once she was inside the house—until the next trip. She'd always been loaded down with presents; fascinating toys, candies and souvenirs for Tad and me.

'I remember once . . .' She stopped and her voice abruptly hardened as she remembered the realities of the current situation. 'Well, that's neither here nor there. Trouble is, you're there—and the sooner you get back here, the better.'

'Yes.' I returned to the present, too. 'What time is it there? Ada, did I wake you up?'

'It doesn't matter. I'm not sleeping much these days, anyhow.'

She would be wearing the chestnut brown velvet robe Buck had given to her last Christmas. I had telephoned on her private line—another of her little independences—so she would be sitting at the rolltop desk she had brought with her when she moved in as housekeeper. The green-shaded lamp wouuld be lit and . . .

I blinked hard and admitted it to myself: I was homesick. Already. I wanted to be back there right now. Perhaps Buck had known me better than I knew myself when he had refused to allow me to participate in the Junior Year Abroad scheme. I had thought that, having lost Tad to a foreign world, he had not dared to trust me to find my feet in another country. Perhaps I had wronged him and he had meant it when he said I was too fragile a plant to take root in foreign soil. Perhaps he had known that I would be swept by this devastating loneliness and uncertainty. Perhaps he had felt it himself, for all his swashbuckling forays to the European Continent.

'I'll be home soon,' I said. 'Maybe tomorrow.'

'And maybe not,' Ada said drily. 'Seems to me your sister-in-law is going to have a fair amount to say about that.'

'I'll bring her with me, if I can. It's her home, too.'

Ada made a throaty little noise, but I knew what she meant. It might not be anyone's home much longer. That was the terrible irony: I was homesick for a home that was already in the process of leaving me. Without Buck, it would never be the same again.

'Oh, Ada—'

'Do your best.' She heard the break in my voice and was quick to cut off the threatened emotion. 'That's all anyone can ask.'

'Yes. Of course I will. The train is leaving soon and it's stopped raining.' I was babbling now, to keep her from tossing down the receiver in her abrupt way and cutting the connection. I didn't want to end this conversation; I would have liked to keep it going until train-time but, with Ada, I knew I hadn't really a hope.

'And it's going to be a fine day here—once the sea mist burns off.' There was a note of grim amusement in her voice. She knew what I was doing; she knew me too well. 'You run along now and be about your business.'

'Ada, wait—'

'Goodbye.' There was a click and the dial tone hummed in my ear. I closed my eyes, trying to cling for a moment longer to the faint link with home.

The dial tone was relentless and insistence, my call was over, I was disconnected. Slowly I replaced the receiver and turned away. The huge station loomed around me, busy and impersonal. I was a traveller, among hundreds of others, just passing through. Home was so far away it might be on a different planet. I was here, and I ought to be about my business—but there was still an hour to kill before train-time.

People moved aside obligingly at the news-stand to allow me a space at the English-language rack. I picked up today's *International Herald-Tribune* and a couple of English news-papers with yesterday's date. I also chose a couple of French magazines; perhaps I could brush up on the language during the train ride.

Linger as I might over my choices, there was still the best

part of an hour to kill before departure time. I picked up a chocolate bar, hoping Madame would appreciate my trying the local speciality—if only she knew. Then what must have been another speciality assailed my nostrils—something smelled very good somewhere.

I followed my nose along a side corridor, past a bar which seemed to be going full blast, even at that hour. Europeans obviously had none of the American inhibitions about suitable hours for drinking. On the opposite side of the corridor there were several opaque windows, obviously belonging to one long room, and from behind them came the promising sound of clattering cutlery and crockery.

The entrance was at the very end of the corridor. I swung the doors open and stepped into a cafeteria-style restaurant, the source of all those delicious smells.

I took a tray and slid it along the railing. There were the usual arrays of food and drink ready to be selected; overhead, a menu set out the dishes that would be cooked to order. I studied it thoughtfully. I wasn't sure whether there would be a restaurant car on the train and I rather liked the idea of having something hot and hearty. Then I needn't bother lurching through a fast-moving train at all.

The cafeteria was not crowded, so I took my time. Also, no serving person was in sight. It was nice not to feel rushed. I was vaguely aware that one of the customers had crossed over to the counter and was standing behind me, outside the rail. Someone after a second cup of coffee, I presumed. A dangerous assumption.

'We recommend the cheese omelette,' a familiar voice remarked.

'You again!' I swung to face him. 'What are you doing here?'

'Getting a bite to eat before travelling on.' He gave me an injured look. 'And you?'

'Madame?' Someone had arrived to take my order.

'Oh, uh . . . a cheese omelette,' I said automatically and

was immediately irritated with myself. Why couldn't I have chosen something—anything—else?

'It will be a minute. If you will sit down, I will call you.'

'Please join us,' Russ said. 'We'd be delighted.'

From a table across the room, Irma waved to me.

'Is she here, too?'

'People *do* have to eat—and this is a very popular place.'

'It looks it.'

'We're between trains right now. It will get busier as the day wears on.'

Irma started to rise. I gave up, waved back and walked over to their table. Russ collected three cups of coffee and followed me—not for the first time, perhaps.

'Hey, this is great!' Irma was far more enthusiastic than I was. 'I wasn't sure I was going to run into you again. What are you doing here?'

'We've just been through that routine.' Russ set down his tray and distributed cups of coffee. 'Like me, she's travelling on from here.' He sat down and gave me a look that was just too innocent. 'I'm heading for Luxembourg. I've always wanted to see it, ever since I used to listen to my mother's LP of *Call Me Madam* when I was a kid.'

I choked over my first sip of coffee.

'Be careful, it's hot.' Irma helpfully thumped my back.

'I'm really looking forward to it.' He smiled at me blandly. 'Where are you heading?'

I took another sip of the scalding coffee. It seemed more tactful than blurting out, 'None of your business!' Through the steam, I peered at him suspiciously. He had volunteered the information, so why did it leave me feeling as though I had just been the target of a pre-emptive strike?

'I wish I was going someplace else,' Irma complained. 'I'm stuck in this crummy town until my jerk of a son-in-law comes to get me.'

That was a relief. I had begun to fear that we were mounting another expedition. All tourists together.

'On the other hand—' Irma brightened. 'Maybe I could come along for one of them day trips. Where did you say you were going?'

I hadn't said and didn't want to. I had the uneasy feeling that Russ already knew. But how could he have known? I hadn't known myself until Inga telephoned a couple of hours ago.

Back at the food counter, someone shouted in our direction. It could only mean that my omelette was ready.

'I'll get it—' Russ leaped to his feet.

'No, no!' I was already standing. 'I want a couple of other things, too. I'll get it.' I moved off firmly.

Not to make a complete liar of myself, I collected a fresh cup of coffee and a goopy pastry dripping with jam and frosting. When I got back to the table, they were both sitting as though they had fallen into a state of suspended animation.

'Hey, that looks good!' My arrival brought Irma back to life. 'I didn't see that when I was there. Are there any more?'

'Lots. They must have just put them out for the luncheon trade. I didn't see them, either, when I was first there.'

'I'll be right back.' She moved more rapidly than I had yet seen her move.

'Where *did* you say you were going?' Russ didn't give me time to sit down. I suspected he wanted to know the answer before Irma was back to hear it.

'I didn't but—' I surrendered—'I'm going to Luxembourg, too.'

'Fine. Then we can travel together.'

'I'm a bad travelling companion,' I warned. 'I've got an armload of magazines and I don't like to talk.'

'I'd rather watch the scenery go past, myself.' He smiled. 'We'll get along just fine.'

'Maybe.' I attacked my omelette with more force than was necessary. I didn't want his company, but I decided that I'd rather know where he was than wonder where he was going to turn up next. And, as for Irma . . .

'Tell her you're going to Switzerland.' He might have been reading my mind, but I looked up and saw that Irma was already heading back to us. 'That's too far for her day trip.'

But Irma appeared to have forgotten her curiosity about my destination. The subject didn't arise again throughout the remainder of our meal. Instead, we were treated to a lengthy analysis of Great Pastries I Have Eaten. This one just missed the Top Ten.

'You're sure you wouldn't put it higher than that?' Russ egged her on. 'Maybe you ought to have another one—just to be sure you judged fairly.'

'That's not a bad idea.' She put both hands on the table and pushed herself to her feet. 'They had one with a peach half on it. That might have been even better. I had a hard time choosing.'

'You owe it to yourself to check it out,' Russ said. 'You'd always regret it, if you didn't.'

'You're right.' She nodded decisively and ambled off.

'Quick!' Russ grabbed my arm and pulled me to my feet. 'Let's go while she's distracted. We can do without her waving us goodbye.' I didn't hesitate.

'Time for our trains!' Russ called out as we dashed past her.

'Okay.' She took our desertion calmly. 'Have a nice time.' She turned back to her contemplation of the pastry counter.

Russ seemed disinclined to slow down, even when we were well away from the cafeteria. He hurried me down the corridor, across the main concourse and up the stairs leading to our platform. I was out of breath when we got there.

A funny little train with a snub-nosed engine was waiting at the platform. I started towards it.

'Not that one.' Russ held me back. 'Over here—' He gestured towards the shining rails below the empty platform on the other side.

'But I thought you said—'

'I was stretching the truth a bit to get away from our friend. We have about five minutes to wait. It will pass quickly.'

I wasn't so sure. I was beginning to think that perhaps he was another friend I would be glad to get away from. Now that I had safely escaped from Irma, he no longer looked like the lesser of two evils. He was beginning to look pretty evil on his own account.

I looked around to see if I could find an excuse to slip away. It didn't look too hopeful. Several uninterested people loitered along our platform; they didn't even look interested in catching their train, so why should I think they might be interested in helping me? On the other platform, doors slammed, whistles shrilled, and announcements in every language except English seemed to indicate that the train was about to depart. A sudden shriek from the train made me jump.

'Nothing changes,' Russ said. 'Ever read any 1930's memoirs? They describe European train whistles as being: "like the shriek of an elderly French spinster who has suddenly been pinched".'

I giggled—and instantly hated myself for it.

The elderly French spinster yelped again and the train slowly slid away from the platform, which now seemed windswept and deserted, standing between the two empty tracks. The passengers who were still waiting for their train stood out conspicuously now.

That is, they would be conspicuous if some of them weren't skulking behind pillars. The yellow *Vertrek/Depart* timetables were posted on several pillars, very sensibly at eye-level, so that people studying them were visible from the waist down.

Why do people imagine they're anonymous just because their faces can't be seen? How many pairs of bare-legged hikers carrying backpacks decorated with the Canadian maple leaf do they think there can be roaming around Brussels in late September? For that matter, wasn't there also something very familiar about that pair of tweed trousers over there behind yet another time-tabled pillar? I suddenly found I wasn't so anxious to part company with Russ, after all. *Better the devil you know* . . .

'Cold?' he asked, as I involuntarily shuddered.

'No, just someone walking over my grave, I guess,' I said —and immediately wished I hadn't. I shuddered again.

'Here comes the train,' Russ said encouragingly, as there was a hysterical whoop in the distance. 'You'll soon be inside and comfortable.'

I doubted that. Not if everyone else was going to pile into the train, too. Was it really possible that Luxembourg was such a popular destination?

I took a deep breath and told myself not to be paranoiac. The train's final destination was deep in Germany; Luxembourg was just one of the stops along the way. It was quite possible that these people were bound for the end of the line —or would get off at one of the other stops. I could not quite convince myself that I believed it.

The train braked to a halt, a door right in front of us. Very convenient—try making something of that. If I could cast the engineer into some sort of conspiracy, that really *would* be paranoia.

Russ stepped forward and opened the door for me. I noticed that he did it without releasing his grip on my arm. Did he think I was going to run away from him? Without demur, I got into the carriage and took a window seat beside the platform. I wanted to see which carriages the others got into.

There was something else I wanted to see, too. I wanted to see whether there was someone else standing somewhere along the platform, watching. Or whether someone would dash up the stairs at the last moment and hurl himself into the train.

I could not believe that we could be on the same Continent and that Tad would not try in some way to make contact with me.

Perhaps I was not the only one who could not believe that. Was I being followed because these people believed I would lead them to Tad? Or to Inga?

## CHAPTER 9

She had Old Buck's blood in her, all right.

Russ watched Hope as she spotted the followers and began trying to puzzle it out. He couldn't fault her for not being able to; he hadn't cracked it himself yet—and he had been aware of it for a lot longer than she had.

For that matter, he hadn't figured out her angle yet, either. Why had she dropped everything and raced off to Europe when her grandfather might die at any minute? And why had she promptly collected the sort of tail that usually followed a major celebrity or a Mafia boss? What had the lady been up to just before her abrupt departure?

He doubted Artie's theory. There was unlikely to be another case like that of the socialite who had stabbed her lover to death, locked the body in a closet and flown off to Europe where she had indulged in a mammoth shopping spree, undeterred by the fact that she was heavily pregnant by her deceased lover. It was not the sort of crime that led to carbon copies.

At least, this one wasn't pregnant—unless it was in the very early stages. But who were all these people following her? The police? Or other interested parties? Was this the sort of case that could engender the sort of headlines that earlier case had produced?

The platform emptied rapidly as brisk announcements in several languages were issued over the loudspeaker. The

Canadian hikers vanished into the carriage ahead; the bearded scholar into the carriage behind. They were neatly boxed in. The elderly French spinster whooped indignantly again and the train slid away from the platform. They were on their way.

She smiled at him tentatively, then opened one of her magazines and became absorbed in it.

No, he refused to believe it possible that she had left behind her a bleeding body stuffed into a closet. Nor was it likely that she had slipped something into the old boy's soup to hasten his demise. News of Buck Bradstone's death would be featured worldwide. Not so prominently as in his heyday, perhaps, but it would still rate a corner of most front pages. The Stock Market, too, would reverberate; again, not with the massive panic-stricken plunge that would have ensued twenty years ago, but there would still definitely be a hiccough or two. No, Buck was still alive. So, nothing on her conscience, but plenty on her mind.

The magazine slipped to half-mast, then lay open and unheeded in her lap. She stared out of the window and did not seem to notice when the city scenes gave way to the dark walls of a tunnel. She didn't even blink when the train charged out of the darkness into daylight again and roared through countryside and forest.

Something very much on her mind.

From behind his paper, he watched her expressionless face as the train glided through some of the most historic territory in Europe. Unnoticing, she stared at small wayside stations with names that had marked the course of the First World War. What was that to her? She hadn't been born then. She was too young—they both were—to have known either world war and been marked by it. Their scars came from subsequent 'local conflicts' and 'peace-keeping actions'. Whatever you called them, men still died.

His own father had died in the closing days of the Korean Conflict, shortly before Russ had been born, leaving his mother an embittered widow with two small children and another on the way. His mother had never been able to come to terms with the fact that a man could have successfully survived the full-scale warfare of the D-Day Invasion and been killed in a 'peace-keeping action' that had never been officially designated as a war, simply because he had committed the basic error of remaining on the Naval Reserve List and been called back to duty when the Korean Conflict broke out. She had done her best to raise her children as pacifists. She had hated it when Russ had become a foreign correspondent, fearing always that he would be sent into danger zones. Bullets and bombs didn't differentiate between active participants and neutral observers. He would surely die in some stinking hellhole with a name no Christian could pronounce.

She had been right and she had been wrong. Twice death had missed him by inches in just the sort of place she had prophesied. He had seen his friends die because their car had swerved to avoid a scraggy mongrel dog—and gone straight over a landmine. Or because they had lagged behind the main company to reload a camera, or strayed off course to get a better shot—and got the kind they hadn't expected. He'd been lucky—also careful. Or perhaps it was just that the one with his number on it hadn't come along yet.

In the end, neither of them had been able to say, 'I told you so.' While he was on a final assignment in the Third World, his mother had died suddenly and unexpectedly, carrying the seed of her own destruction in a thinning arterial wall which had abruptly burst. For a while after that he had not been so careful, but it hadn't mattered. He had survived.

Ironically, his next assignment had been to the safety of a European Bureau. The only danger there had been cirrhosis of the liver. He'd enjoyed it, though, feeling that he'd earned the right to a few fat years after so many lean ones. The summons to return Stateside had not pleased him.

Was that why he had seized on the first excuse to rush back? Artie was right—the Chiefs were going to be furious. He hadn't even got as far as leaving the airport, much less reporting to the newspaper office.

Well, either the Bradstone Heiress was going to be the biggest rabbit he'd ever pulled out of the hat, or he was going to be looking for a new job. If he'd annoyed the heirarchy sufficiently, it might be both.

The train pulled into a station with a haunting name and stopped. Hope stirred suddenly and turned to him.

'Isn't this . . .?' She sounded startled, as though she had never made the connection before. 'I mean, are these *the* places . . .?'

'That's right. The First World War and part of the Second was fought over this territory. We're deep in the Ardennes. They're all here in Belgium, you know: Ypres, Mons, Flanders Field. They call this country The Crossroads of Europe—and most of the invading armies of the past centuries fought their way through it. Waterloo is here, too.'

'I hadn't realized—'

'For a tourist, you haven't done your homework. Most tourists read a couple of books about the places they're heading for before they begin their journey.'

'This was a sudden impulse.' Her face was shuttered again; she began to turn away. 'I didn't have time for any reading.'

'Probably just as well,' he said quickly. If she got upset enough, there was nothing to prevent her from getting up and moving to another carriage. 'This way, you're coming to it with a freshness of mind and eye. No preconceived notions, no one else's thoughts and prejudices cluttering up your mind.'

She was still frowning slightly, but her face had begun to clear. 'I wouldn't have read that part of the travel guide, anyway. I hate wars.'

'Not many people are very keen on them. Apart from the military—and some politicians.'

'I hate politicians, too.'

'Very wise of you. Half-crazed empire builders have accounted for most of the troubles of the world.' He immediately regretted saying that; if ever anyone could be counted an empire builder, Old Buck could. Even though it had been a business empire, rather than a political one.

'They have a lot to answer for—if they ever do.' Fortunately, she didn't seem to make the connection.

'Yes. Practically every mile of this country has been drenched in human blood.' Since she was being forthcoming, he decided on a calculated risk. 'I don't think there's another country with a record like it—except perhaps for Vietnam.'

Her face froze. 'Who are you?' she demanded abruptly.

'A friend, believe me, I mean you no harm.' He'd struck a nerve. 'I'm on your side.' It was true. Whatever the story, he would handle it with more tact and sympathy than a lot of others he could name. He would present her to the public in the best possible light.

'I might have known it! Buck sent you, didn't he? He didn't trust me on my own, after all, did he? He had to send along a nursemaid!'

'You mustn't blame Mr Bradstone.' Over the years, he had become an expert at the indirect lie. Although annoyed, she would be more willing to accept him as Buck's emissary than as a reporter out for a story. 'It's only natural. He wants to take care of you . . . for as long as he can.'

'I suppose so.' Her tone was sulky, but her eyes brimmed with sudden tears. That was a pretty good indication of how much longer Buck was expected to be able to go on taking care of anybody. So, why *had* she left him at a time like this? What was the great attraction in Luxembourg?

She turned her head away, staring out of the window. They were close to the border now; stacks of peeled logs were piled high alongside the tracks and beside the fences of the farms they passed.

'We're nearly there,' he said. 'It won't be long now.'

'I suppose you know this territory quite well.' Buck wouldn't have sent someone who didn't.

'Well enough,' he admitted. There had been trips to cover special EEC hearings, and the inevitable international rock stars who had given concerts on Radio Luxembourg. 'They call it the Green Heart of Europe.'

'When I want the guided tour, I'll tell you!'

'Sorry.' Was she going to be snobbish because she thought he was just one of the hired hands? She hadn't seemed that sort.

'Anyway—' If he was going to be marked down as one of the Bradstone lackeys, let it be clear that he was an independent-type lackey. 'We've just crossed the border. Welcome to the Grand Duchy of Luxembourg!'

She started to open her shoulder-bag.

'No, no,' he said. 'You don't need to tip me. It's all part of the service.'

'I was looking for my passport,' she snarled.

'Not necessary. There's a Customs Union between Belgium and Luxembourg. No papers necessary. They have an open border.'

'Have they?' She looked as though something she had been puzzling over had suddenly made sense to her.

'And you can use your Belgian francs in Luxembourg— although the currency arrangement doesn't work the other way round.'

She didn't bother to answer. She was deep in thought again.

# CHAPTER 10

According to the timetable, we should be arriving at Luxembourg City station in ten minutes. The first priority was going to be to get rid of this clown.

Buck had meant well, but I couldn't help being furious. At myself, if no one else. I should have suspected something of the sort. No wonder Buck had taken my departure so calmly; no wonder Ada had been so complacent.

Buck's involvement in all the Bradstone Enterprises had, necessarily, diminished over the past few years, but his tentacles could still stretch out to wrap around a likely pawn and set him down to checkmate me. Or just keep check on me. He could not know how disastrous that might be.

Inga was nervous and desperately frightened, perhaps hysterical. If she saw me in the company of some unknown man, she would never approach me. She might even run away and hide again—taking Jan-Carl with her.

I could not risk that. I had to lose this Russ before he lost me Inga and the very reason I was here in the first place. If possible, I had to lose him before we arrived at Luxembourg City station. Inga might be waiting there with Jan-Carl.

And what of the others? The contingent from the *Poisson d'Or*? Maybe they weren't really following me. Maybe they were just people who happened to be travelling in the same direction and were more noticeable because the tourist season had passed its peak and there were not so many around now. Maybe . . .

Maybe they thought I'd lead them to Tad.

Tad had enemies, Inga had said. She believed he had gone into hiding to escape them. If they couldn't find Tad, they might settle for Inga—and Jan-Carl.

Or me. Suddenly, it did not seem so unwise to have an escort—a bodyguard—standing by, after all. Since childhood, I had been aware of the ever present danger of kidnappers. Not to the point of being terrified to move, Buck hadn't wanted that. But a reasonable caution had been instilled in me. I had been taught to be wary of strangers, to always tell the family where I was going, to let them know if my plans for the evening changed—and never to take unnecessary chances.

But some chances had to be taken. With a strange male looming beside me, it was odds on that Inga would take fright again and disappear. Whatever had been happening to her in the years since she had married Tad, she too had learned caution and distrust.

'Look—' I turned to Russ as the city came into view. 'Can we strike a bargain?'

'I don't know.' He considered the idea uneasily. 'What sort of bargain?'

'I have to meet someone here. If they see you, they won't show up. Can you keep out of the way for a couple of hours?'

'Well . . .' His eyes were wary. I could almost feel sorry for him. If he lost me and anything happened, Buck would be infuriated enough to crush him. On the other hand, I was one of the Bradstone heirs. If he didn't go along with me, I might be vindictive enough to have him dismissed when we got home. Either way, his future with Bradstone Enterprises was on the line.

'You can keep watching me, if you want to,' I bargained. 'Just don't let anyone see you—and keep your distance. I've got to appear to be alone. It's vital.'

'Well, I suppose . . .' He wasn't happy about it.

'Fine.' I took it for consent—he had no other choice. 'While you're staying out of my way, you might keep an eye on anyone else who gets off at this stop and make sure they look as if they had legitimate business here.' I didn't want to mention the Canadian hikers or the bearded professor specifically. I would look foolish if none of them alighted here. But, if they did, I wanted to know that they were under surveillance.

'You're expecting trouble?' He took me up on it too quickly, a bit nervously. Buck should have opted for a professional minder instead of one of the company's junior executives; but time had been short and I guess he'd done the best he could.

'Not necessarily trouble. I'd just like to make sure I'm not being followed.'

'And . . . if you are?'

'Then I want to know about it.' And then I would decide what to do next. One step at a time, however.

'Okay, I'll see to that.' *I can do that much*, was implied. Again, I wondered just how useful he would be in the event of a genuine emergency. Not that I was expecting one, but Inga seemed to be.

'Let me get off the train first,' I said, as it slowed for the station. 'You can follow later—a lot later.'

He gave me an oblique look suggesting that, if he left it too late, he might be carried along to the next station—and was that what I really had in mind? It seemed that we had arrived at a fine situation of mutual mistrust.

It was, of course, expecting too much to find Inga waiting at the station. I could only cross my fingers that she was somewhere nearby, watching while she made sure I was alone.

As I had suspected, both the hikers and the professor alighted, too. Russ kept to our agreement and swung off the train just as the whistles began blowing to signal its departure.

I became urgently absorbed in hunting for something at the bottom of my shoulder-bag, allowing everyone to precede me through the ticket barrier. No one even glanced at me or seemed disposed to linger. No one was loitering in the waiting-room when I passed the barrier itself.

Not even Inga. I stood beside a timetable and surveyed the area as thoroughly as possible. All clear. I moved closer to the exit to check the street outside.

I was just about to step outside when I spotted them: the two hikers, just at the periphery of my field of vision, unfolding a map and hunching over it.

At the same time, the bearded man, frowning as though he had forgotten something, was returning to the station. Russ was nowhere in sight—he had already done too good a job of concealing himself.

I stepped back hastily and looked around. There was a Ladies Room at one side of the station; I dived for it and was safely inside before the bearded man had entered the station. He might suspect where I had disappeared to, but he could not follow me. He could only try to outwait me.

And he would have some wait! To my delight, I found that this Ladies Room had some of the comforts of home: showers and bathtubs. I could kill time quite pleasantly here and perhaps hide myself among the debarking passengers from a later train. I still had that ratty old wig in my holdall—they hadn't seen me in that—and I could change into my other outfit. If necessary, when I got to the shops in the town, I could buy different clothes to further confuse my followers. I suspected that they were not accustomed to trailing a chameleon—and I was prepared to change my colours at every possible stopping place.

Besides, it would be dark before long. That would help, too. I doubted that these characters—whoever they were— would know this area any better than I did. Not if the way they were poring over that map was anything to judge by.

There was always the chance that they were all quite legitimate tourists and Inga's paranoia had infected me. After all, Luxembourg was a popular tourist destination.

*Not that popular at this time of the year*, a little voice said within my head.

But other people had also got off the train here. People who had nothing to do with Tad or Inga—

*That you know of* . . .

I cut short the schizophrenic argument and walked over to the big mirror. The first thing I saw was my own name scrawled in lipstick across the top of it.

'HOPE—TRINFO.'

'Vandals! Vandals!' Even as I stared at it, the attendant bustled up with a soapy cloth and attacked it. 'Always the graffiti! Can they not remember who they are if they do not write their names on every surface?'

But it was my name—in my sister-in-law's unmistakable spiky handwriting. A message, could I but decode it.

'Terrible!' I agreed and slipped into the nearest cubicle before she had time to note my appearance. Inside, I donned the blonde wig and, after a suitable interval, emerged to make arrangements for a hot bath.

Although I took my time over my bath, I kept my eye on my watch and was dressed, bewigged and ready to join the outgoing passengers when the next train from Germany stopped at the station.

Sandwiched between two hefty *Hausfraus*, I got clear of the station and looked around. None of the men I had worried about was in sight. Perhaps I had worried unnecessarily and they had all gone about their lawful business. By now, Russ ought to be able to tell me, but I couldn't see him, either.

What I did see was a Tourist Information Centre. Suddenly, Inga's message made sense: HOPE—TRINFO. Tourist Information. She might be waiting for me there—or she might have left another, less cryptic, message.

I slipped away from my unwitting guardians and crossed over to the building. Inside, a sprinkling of newly-arrived tourists from the train were milling about, selecting brochures from the display racks and lining up for more specialized information from one of the attendants on duty behind the counter.

I browsed along the racks of brochures until the first rush was out of the way, then approached the information counter myself.

'Oh yes, here is your message.' A sealed envelope was handed to me. I retreated to a quiet corner to open it and read Inga's latest instructions. If she was going to direct me to yet another destination, I was prepared to be very annoyed.

However, it seemed that I had reached the end of the trail—or almost.

Dear Hope,
We are at the *Hôtel du Monde, Rue Capellen*, off Boulevard Roosevelt. We wait here for you. Do not be followed. Jan-Carl is anxious to meet you. He sends love and kisses.
Inga.

There was a small crudely-drawn map; I assumed the one big X on it was the location of the hotel and not a kiss from Jan-Carl. Other than that, it was clear enough and I tried to memorize it before tucking it into my jacket pocket and setting out.

It was twilight and the streetlamps were beginning to flicker on. I sauntered in the direction of the Boulevard Roosevelt, trying to act like a typical tourist and hoping that my frequent pauses and turnings would look like someone appreciating the scenery to the full and not as though I were trying to check on whether I was being followed.

The scenery was, even in the growing dusk, spectacular. I had not realized that Luxembourg was built on two levels, with great bridges spanning deep ravines. Hundreds of feet below, the lower section of the city was marked out by streetlamps and rows of houses, heavily wooded areas and a river running along its bed. At one point, I looked over the railing of a bridge and shuddered at the sheer drop to the valley below.

'There are over sixty bridges in the capital city,' a voice said behind me. 'It is claimed that one cannot reach anywhere in the city without crossing a bridge.'

I whirled, thinking they had caught up with me, but found a solemn man squinting at his guidebook and relaying the information to his female companion, who appeared far more interested in the beckoning lights of the shops on the far side of the bridge.

As I was myself. I felt too isolated and vulnerable on the bridge. A cold wind had sprung up and I wondered if people were ever blown off the bridges to crash into the gorge so far below. It was not a comfortable thought and I quickened my steps, breathing more easily when I achieved the security of solid ground. The wind was not so high here, either.

Lighted shop windows displayed enticing luxury goods, delicious fragrances from bakeries and restaurants suddenly reminded me of how many hours it had been since my brunch in Brussels station. Then I saw the street sign for Boulevard Roosevelt and forgot everything else.

The *Hôtel du Monde* was another anonymous, secretive-looking building. Inga seemed to have a penchant for them. Or was it Tad? *Private Hotel*, the sign specified beneath the name and it looked very private indeed. I was relieved to find that the door opened to my touch.

The reception desk was untended, the lobby dimly lit. I looked around uncertainly. Something stirred in the shadows; I whirled to face it.

'Hope?' A slight figure moved forward cautiously, eyes darting about, looking for danger at every step. 'Hope, it is you, Yes?'

'Inga!' She was much thinner than she had been in the last photograph I had seen. Her deep blue eyes had retreated into their sockets and dark circles made them appear deeper.

Worry lines were etched into her forehead and along the sides of her mouth.

'Inga—' I started towards her impulsively. 'How nice to meet you at last!'

'Yes.' She shrank back before I could touch her. 'We have not much time. Come upstairs.' She turned and led the way towards a flight of stairs, ignoring the elevator at the end of the lobby.

'You are truly Hope?' She paused at the first landing and looked back at me doubtfully. 'Your hair—'

'It's a wig.' I pulled it off and smoothed it before putting it into my holdall. It had been useful to me so often, I was prepared to treat it with more respect.

'I thought—' I hesitated, unwilling to feed her fears by admitting that I thought I had been followed from Brussels.

'That is good.' She did not require an explanation as to why I might be trying to disguise myself; it seemed natural to her. She turned and started up the next flight of stairs. 'It is good, too, that you do not wear it to meet Jan-Carl. He has seen your pictures. It would frighten him to see you looking different and, I think, he is frightened enough already.'

*So are you.* I did not say it. I settled for: 'You seem to have been having a difficult time lately.'

'Ah yes,' she sighed. 'There are trolls under every bridge.'

'And you've certainly picked a place with enough bridges for them,' I muttered under my breath. Then I needed all my breath as we mounted yet another flight of stairs. What did she have against elevators?

'Shhh!' At last, we were on the top landing and Inga waved me to silence, although all I was doing by this time was gasping for breath. She tapped on a door and called out something in Swedish. After a long pause, the door opened slowly.

'Quickly!' She caught my wrist and drew me inside, not very gently. The door slammed behind us and she jumped and said something that sounded as though it might be a swear word.

'For heaven's sake, Inga—' I rubbed my wrist. 'Did you have to dislocate my—? Then I saw him and lost all track of what I had intended to say.

'Jan-Carl?' Of course it was. It could be no one else. 'Jan-Carl!'

He backed away as I moved forward to embrace him. It had been the wrong move. All children were shy. He had never seen me before and I had moved too fast. It would take time for us to become acquainted.

'How do you do, Jan-Carl?' I held out my hand formally. 'I'm your Aunt Hope.'

He gave a quick uncertain smile. For a fleeting instant, his tiny fine-boned hand rested in mine. Politely but firmly, he nodded to me and moved to stand beside his mother— not quite hiding behind her skirt, but ready to move there, if necessary. I had forgotten how young he was—and that European children are less sophisticated than their American counterparts.

'He's so like Tad!'

'Yes.' Inga frowned again, not entirely happy with my verdict. 'Also, he is much like *my* brother when a child.' It was a clear reminder that the bloodlines of two families were flowing through Jan-Carl's delicate blue veins.

Jan-Carl shot me a sudden amused, triumphant look and I caught my breath. Buck! It was the same expression I had seen so often on Buck's face. I was certain then that I was doing the right thing. There was more Bradstone in him than any of Inga's Scandinavian line; he belonged back in New England with us.

And soon. I looked at Inga and saw her read the urgent message in my eyes.

'Yes,' she agreed. 'We must hurry.'

'I'm ready,' I prodded her. 'So far as I'm concerned, we can walk out that door right now and head for the airport.'

'Ah!' She frowned. 'It is not that easy.'

Somehow, I'd had a feeling it wouldn't be. 'Why not?'

'There are . . . complexities.'

'Complications?' Something else I might known. Inga's entire life seemed to consist of complications.

'*Ja.*' She looked down uneasily at Jan-Carl. His bright blue eyes returned her gaze. 'I must explain.'

'I wish you would. I'd really appreciate it if someone would explain something to me. I've been stumbling from pillar to post in the dark for days now.'

'Pillar post?' Inga looked alarmed. 'You have not been posting letters?'

The bright blue gaze shifted to me and I tried to smile at my nephew, uncomfortably aware that even a seven-year-old knew more of what was going on than I did.

'Hope, those letters. To whom—?'

'For heaven's sake, Inga, there weren't any letters. I didn't post anything. It was just a figure of speech.'

'Oh.' She did not look reassured.

'Inga, you're wasting time!' Or was she playing for time? She had been evading me, stalling and temporizing, from the moment I had arrived. Why?

'I do not mean to.' She was tearful. 'Truly, I do not, Hope.'

Jan-Carl gave me a hostile look. I was making his mother cry. If I wasn't careful, he would begin to think of me as an enemy. Heaven knows, the poor child appeared to have encountered enough of them in his short span.

'All right, Inga,' I said soothingly, 'don't get upset. But we *must* get the first flight out—' I stopped; she was shaking her head again. I fought down an impulse to shake *her*.

'We cannot,' she said. 'They will be watching the airport.'

There *They* were again. I glanced at Jan-Carl. But I was not so disposed to dismiss Inga's fears now that I had picked up a few *Theys* of my own.

'Jan-Carl,' I said, 'why don't you run away and play, or

something? I want to talk to your mother.'

He ignored me.

'Jan-Carl!' Inga spoke sharply, her tone told me more than the Swedish words she used, but Jan-Carl heeded them. Reluctantly, he turned and marched into the bathroom, shutting the door firmly behind him.

'Now we have a moment to speak,' Inga said. 'He will be ready to leave when he comes out.'

For the first time, I noticed that there was only one small suitcase standing beside the door.

'Inga, you've got to come, too. I can't go home without you.'

'I am all right,' she said stubbornly. 'I must stay to help Tad.'

'What sort of help does he need? Why? Where is he?' It was too much; I shouldn't have asked so many questions so fast. She was shaking her head again. I was forming the opinion that my dear sister-in-law did not like questions— any questions at all.

'Inga, you've got to tell me *something!*'

She glanced wistfully towards the closed door and I could read her expression: If only Jan-Carl would come back, I would have to stop asking all these questions.'

'Inga, what's wrong? Is Tad in trouble with the police?"

'No.' Her face cleared slightly. 'Not the police . . . not yet.'

'Yet . . . All right.' I heard in my voice the weary resignation I had heard in Buck's voice when he was faced with a certain type of crisis. 'How much will it take to buy him out of this trouble?'

'You do not understand. There is not that much money in the world.'

'There's always that much money—if you know how to get it.' The cynical thought occurred to me that it might be Tad himself behind this, trying to play his family for as much as he could get out of them. If so, he had coached

Inga well. She seemed genuinely terrified.

'You Americans!' She was also furious. 'You think money can buy anything!'

'Usually, it can. Why won't it this time?'

'Because They prefer revenge!' She spat it out, then looked terrified again.

'Now we're getting something. Don't stop there. Who are *They?*'

'I do not know. I am not sure. Please, go away and take Jan-Carl with you—to safety.'

'Are you telling me Tad has crossed the Mafia?'

'No, no. There are other . . . organizations. People like . . . him.'

'People like himself?' For a moment, I was puzzled, then it became all too clear. Tad had not many peer groups left in the world to which he had disappeared. 'I take it you don't mean expatriates . . . you mean deserters.'

'You must understand. Sweden offered refuge. We have always been neutral. For a long time we did not understand ourselves that there were two kinds. There were the deserters from Vietnam, they were the good ones—most of them. They fled the fighting and killing, they wanted only peace—'

'At any price.' It was a bitter echo of Buck.

'But there were the others. English and Americans who deserted from their forces in Germany. They told us lies about the treatment they had received and the reasons they deserted. We gave them much sympathy and help. Then they began to behave badly and we discovered the truth. They were deserters because they had operated Black Markets and been caught. Or involved in other crimes. They ran away before the Court Martials.'

More deserters. It had never occurred to me that there could be more than one sort of deserter—from more than one army.

'But what did they have to do with Tad?'

'At first, nothing. But . . . he was lonely.'

'He had you and Jan-Carl. That's more than a lot of other ex-soldiers had. He'd made a new life for himself.'

'*Ja*, but we were not enough. My English is good—I teach it sometimes—but it is not the same. The . . . the common memories are important, too. He met these others, then he began seeing them more, staying out nights with them. Sometimes, he brought them to the flat, but I did not like them. Their eyes watched, they made rude jokes, they laughed too loud. They . . . frightened me. Once, Jan-Carl woke up and they frightened him, too. After that, Tad met them outside.'

'Let me get this straight—' I didn't like the conclusion I was drawing as she spoke. 'Are you telling me that Tad got mixed up in some sort of *racket* with these men?'

'I do not *know*.' She frowned. 'But I think, yes. Suddenly, he had more money. The telephone rang late at night and he went out. He would not tell me why.'

'Oh no!' It added up. She was probably right, but it boded ill for my secret hope. Tad, as a youthful deserter, cracking under pressures that had broken older men, might yet be forgiven by Buck if I could arrange a confrontation. But Tad, deliberately mixed up in illegal activities—piling fresh disgrace on the family name if he were caught—was another proposition.

No wonder he was on the run again.

'You think he had some sort of falling out with these men?'

'One night he did not come back.' Inga shrugged. 'I think he is with them. And then the telephones started. They demand to know where he is. They do not believe me when I tell them I do not know. They say if he goes to the police, they will— They make many threats. Then your letter came and I knew you must take Jan-Carl away.'

'I'm taking both of you.' If I said it often enough, maybe I could convince her.

There was a sudden sharp rattling noise. I jumped involuntarily, but it was only the bathroom door opening. Jan-Carl stood there.

'We are ready now,' Inga said.

## CHAPTER 11

With Jan-Carl present, we could talk no more. Silently, Inga picked up the small suitcase beside the door and held out her hand. Jan-Carl came forward and took it, looking at me questioningly.

'Yes,' I said. 'I'm ready, too.' Over his head, my eyes met Inga's with a question of my own.

'We go to the station,' she said. 'There is a train soon. It comes from Cologne and goes to Brussels. You can fly from there.'

'Okay.' I hoped she knew what she was doing. I couldn't see why she thought her enemies would be watching the airport but not the train station. Presumably, she knew something I didn't.

We went down the stairs. I noticed that Jan-Carl did not even expect to use the elevator. He was obviously well attuned to his mother's phobias.

The reception area was still empty. Inga dropped her room key into the slot at the desk with an air of finality. She must already have settled her account, for the room we had left was empty of any personal possessions. And yet she was carrying nothing more than her handbag and Jan-Carl's case. Had she already transferred her belongings to her next bolthole? I was still going to have something to say about that.

She stopped at the door and moved the window curtain aside fractionally, carefully studying the street outside. Jan-Carl stood motionless beside her; he was a very silent child.

Or was he, like his mother, very frightened?

'Yes,' Inga decided. 'We go now.' She opened the door just enough to allow her to slip through; Jan-Carl crowded close behind her. I followed.

Inga avoided the street lights and hurried us from one pool of shadows to another. Now she had me looking over my shoulder.

Jan-Carl murmured something to his mother. The only word I caught was *Trolls*.

On a night like this, it was easy to believe in such things. And we were approaching one of those everlasting bridges.

'Don't be silly, Jan-Carl.' I tried to encourage him. 'Any trolls would have to have wings to get us if they were lurking under *this* bridge!'

Their faces turned to me briefly, but they remained silent. It was not a joking matter. Inga leaned over and said something to Jan-Carl, then took my arm and drew me aside, still deeper into the shadows. I thought she was going to reprove me, but I was wrong.

'Here—' She thrust a small oblong object into my hand. 'Here is Jan-Carl's passport. You will need it. Guard it well.'

'But, Inga, why don't you hold on to it. You're coming with us. I insist.'

'Put it away.' Her tone brooked no argument. 'I—I will join you later. I have things that must be done first.'

'Inga—' I shoved the passport into my shoulder-bag; it was easier than arguing with her. 'I wish I could be sure you know what you're doing.'

'*Ja.*' A car drove past us. In the brief flash of its headlights, I could see her wan smile. 'I wish so, too.'

'Mamma! Mamma!' We had stayed apart talking for too long; Jan-Carl was beside us, reaching for Inga's hand again.

'Jan-Carl!' She knelt suddenly and gathered him into her

arms, holding him tight and speaking in Swedish in a voice that trembled close to tears.

'*Nej!*' He squirmed in her embrace, denying it, denying everything she was saying. '*Nej, Mamma, nej!*'

'*JA! Ja, Jan-Carl!*' She shook him slightly and changed into English for my benefit. 'You must go with your Aunt Hope. She will take care of you. You will go to America. Your father's country. You will like America. I—we both —will come to you soon.'

Jan-Carl glared at me and clutched his mother.

'*Ja!*' She straightened up and spoke to me directly. 'It is all right. He will go with you.' She pressed his cold, unwilling little hand into mine.

'Now we must hurry.' Inga started forward again. 'Or you will miss your train.'

'*Our* train,' I insisted, knowing the battle was already lost.

She gave me a fleeting smile over her shoulder and kept walking.

Did something stir in the shadows just ahead?

Where was Russ? I looked around with increasing indignation. That rising young executive had better rise to this occasion if he intended a continuing career in the family firm. If I could just slip aside and talk to him for a moment . . . brief visions danced through my mind. I couldn't manage it alone but, between the two of us, we could surely overpower Inga and take her with us. A discreet kidnapping, with the best of intentions could not possibly do her any harm.

Unless she was lying to me. Unless she knew where Tad was hiding and was going to him as soon as she had seen us aboard the train. That might explain why she was so sure that *They* would be watching the airport. If Tad had deliberately led them there, acting as decoy while his son escaped by train . . . that could explain a lot of things.

But where was Russ? Was he at the airport, too, following the followers? If so, it would be a very worried man who reported back to his superiors that he had lost the boss's grand-daughter somewhere in Luxembourg.

I followed Inga automatically. Jan-Carl trudged beside me, head down, still reluctantly allowing me to hold his hand; he seemed to have accepted that he had been handed over to me, although he was not happy about it.

We were crossing the bridge now, a cold wind sweeping up from the depths below and curling around us. Inga's skirt fluttered and she bent stubbornly into the wind. Like Jan-Carl, I lowered my head and forged forward. Ahead of us sloped the hill leading down to the station, past rows of shops. Once we were off the bridge, it would be warmer—and brighter. People were walking about, still doing some late shopping. I quickened my steps, heedless of Jan-Carl's short legs. I wanted to be in the midst of the crowd, in a street without shadows. It wasn't far now.

'Here.' Inga halted abruptly as we stepped off the bridge and swung about. 'Take Jan-Carl's suitcase.' She pushed it at me and I caught it mechanically. 'Go straight ahead and you will find the station. I must go back now.'

'Inga, please—'

At the same moment, Jan-Carl lifted his head. '*Nej, Mamma, nej!*' His voice was soft and on the verge of tears. He, too, knew that his plea was hopeless.

'Be a good boy.' She bent and kissed him swiftly. Tears shone in her eyes as she straightened and hurried away, not trusting herself to linger over the farewell.

'Mamma!' He tried to follow her, but I held him back. If he ran off and got lost in the darkness, my whole trip would have been in vain. Together, we stood and watched her hurrying back across the bridge.

She almost made it.

She was three-quarters of the way to safety when figures moved towards her from the opposite end. She stopped and began to back away. There was a crash and a tinkle of falling glass as one of the lights on the bridge shattered. She was in darkness then and the figures were upon her.

'Stay here, Jan-Carl!' I dropped his hand and began to run towards them. The suitcase bumped against my leg. I should have dropped that, too. On the other hand, it might come in useful to swing out at them.

Except that there was no more time. It all happened so fast. The figures converged in one struggling mass. Inga screamed.

Then one figure was detached from the others, lifted high —up and over the parapet.

The second scream died away as Inga disappeared from sight, plunging towards the ravine so far below.

'Mamma!'

Jan-Carl was at my side. After that one agonized cry, he was silent, gripping my hand. Two dark figures turned in our direction and began running towards us.

'*Vi måste springa, Faster Hope. Vi måste gömma oss!*'

I didn't know what he was saying, but the way he tugged at my hand was plain. I was with him; we had no intention of hanging around and waiting until those murderers caught up with us. We began to run back to our side of the bridge.

We had a good head start and, once off the bridge, Jan-Carl pulled me into a side street. I let him lead the way, hoping he had been in the city long enough to have a sense of direction. Anyway, we were back in the shadows and this was no time to start asking questions. I concentrated on trying not to trip as we threaded our way through narrow alleys and down dark streets, past shuttered windows and implacably closed doors. I didn't know if our pursuers were lost, but I certainly was.

When we finally stopped, gasping for breath and too exhausted to run another step, we were deep in unknown territory, but we seemed to be by ourselves. We huddled against a wall, fighting to get our breath under control.

Jan-Carl gasped out something. The only word I caught

was *Mamma*. He pulled at my hand, urging me onwards again.

'Wait a minute,' I protested. 'Let's rest here for a few minutes and try to think what to do next.' I knew what we ought to do—and I knew that we couldn't. Inga was beyond help; going to the police would mean endless delay, red tape and questions I couldn't answer. We might be stuck here for days—and that was unthinkable. Inga's time had already run out. Buck's was running out fast. If he was to see Jan-Carl, we had to get away.

'Mamma . . .' His voice blurred into a little sniffle.

'Oh, Jan-Carl—' I knelt beside him. 'I'm sorry. I'm so sorry.' I rummaged in my shoulder bag and found a crumpled paper handkerchief. 'Here—'

'*Jag ar en stor pojke!*' He threw it aside angrily. '*Stora pojkar gråter inte.*'

Before I could absorb this, he pushed me away, then grabbed my arm and pulled at me urgently. '*Mamma—*' he insisted. '*Jag vill till Mamma!*'

'Oh, Jan-Carl!' I realized what he had been trying to do. I had been vaguely aware that we had been running downhill most of the time. We must be deep in the ravine now. He was trying to get to his mother . . . his mother's body.

'Jan-Carl, no! Darling, it's no use. She can't have survi—I mean, we can't help her.' I could not let him see what she must look like after that fall. He would have enough nightmares for the rest of his life without that.

'Come on, Jan-Carl.' I tried to turn him away from the valley, to lead him back towards the upper town.

'*Nej!*' He dug in his heels and would not be budged.

'Oh, Jan-Carl.' I looked at him despairingly. The only thing to do was pick him up and carry him, but I couldn't manage that and the suitcase and holdall.

*Where was Russ?* I was suddenly, irrationally furious. I needed his help now and where was he? Together, we could have managed. By myself . . .

'Jan-Carl, please be reasonable.'
*'De dödade min Mamma.'* He looked up at me stubbornly.
*'De vil döda oss allihopa.'*
'Oh no!' I met his gaze with growing consternation. This was an additional complication I had never anticipated.

It had never occurred to me that Tad's son would not be able to speak English.

## CHAPTER 12

Russ raised his head and immediately realized that he had overestimated his athletic ability. Sharp pains, bright flashes of light, nausea, dizziness—he had the lot. He never should have taken that last drink—that last half-dozen drinks. He shook his head—which was an even worse mistake—and sank back into unconsciousness.

When he surfaced again, some time later, he remembered that he hadn't had a drink since yesterday—and then it had only been one bottle of Stella Artois. He lay very still, contemplating this realization, and became aware that he was lying on something hard and cold. Furthermore, there was an icy wind circling around him. He took several deep breaths and forced his eyes open.

As he had suspected, he was lying on the ground. Rather, on an unevenly paved surface, large lumps of which were digging into his back. It was pitch black, the only lights were the rockets and starbursts still going off behind his eyes. A few more deep breaths and he rolled over on an elbow and tried to lever himself upwards. That was another mistake. He fell back—nothing but mistakes—his head thumped against something hard and dizziness overwhelmed him again.

Next time he regained consciousness, he was craftier. He lay doggo until the fireworks display faded out behind his retinas;

he breathed deeply until his breathing became so normal that he was unaware of it. When he began to move, it was so slowly that his muscles took the strain without noticing. Carefully, cautiously, he raised himself to a sitting position and rested there before launching himself on further exertions.

So far so good. If only he could find a wall, or a tree, or something he could prop himself up against for another hour or so, he might eventually hope to find himself upright some time before dawn.

*Hope!* He lurched to his feet and stood there swaying as memory reasserted itself. *Where was she? Where was he? What had happened?*

Rockets flared, starbursts released showers of shooting stars in all colours of the rainbow; it was the fourth of July all over again. Except that it was September—he hung on to that. *It's a long, long time . . . from May to December . . . and the days grow short . . . when you reach September . . .*

September . . . Luxembourg . . . not much time . . . Hope . . . concussion . . .?

He found the side of a building and leaned against it. His head spun like a roulette wheel, then abruptly cleared. He shouldn't crowd his luck by doing anything wildly melodramatic—like walking—but scenes and impressions were beginning to filter through to him.

Good. So he probably didn't have amnesia. Probably. It was supposed to be the last couple of hours just before the accident that were lost with amnesia.

What had happened to him was no accident.

It was all coming back now. On the train . . . the plea from the Bradstone heiress—with the lightly veiled threat behind it (and heaven help the junior executives in Bradstone Enterprises when she got her hands on the reins) . . . his own amusement at her mistake and recognition that this would be the best way to gain her confidence—and the growing realization that there might be a bigger story here than he had ever imagined.

Because she was right; she was being followed. And her strategy wasn't bad, either. It had been a laugh to see her disappear into the Ladies and watch the discomfort of her followers as they realized they could not follow her there, and then their growing fury and concern as she did not re-emerge. The bearded booklover had retreated at that point, but the two hikers had hung on.

They had been caught on the hop when the train from Germany discharged its passengers and she had mingled with them, wearing that ratty wig and a different outfit. Too bad she hadn't been able to change her shoes, holdall and shoulder-bag. It's the little things that give the game away.

Moving away from the cover of the crowd hadn't helped, either. By the time she left the Tourist Information Centre, they'd spotted her again.

This time, they'd played it cagey, letting her get almost out of sight before they started after her. Russ had trailed a long way after them, occasionally wondering uneasily where the bearded man had disappeared to. More by luck than judgement, he suspected, Hope had lost them all.

One moment she had been approaching a crossroads, then there had been a sudden convergence of traffic. When the traffic had cleared, she was gone. From the way the hikers stared at the departing tail lights, they obviously thought that she had slipped into one of the vehicles and been driven off to some rendezvous.

Nevertheless, they had remained close to the spot where they had last seen her. In a move that had Russ weak with envy, they had pulled sandwiches and plastic bottles from their backpacks and settled down on a bench for an impromptu picnic. Why hadn't he had the foresight to pick up some supplies along the way?

Remembering, his stomach rumbled in protest, but there was nothing to eat around here. He pushed himself away from the building and tried to stand without support. The wobble in his legs provided a new worry: could he walk unaided?

He had to; there were things that he must do. In just another minute, he would remember what they were. His head had begun a deep steady throbbing. He raised his hand to the source—the base of his skull—and his fingers winced away from the large lump he found rising there.

That was it: he had been ambushed and attacked. Struck down from behind. Left in the gutter to live or die—they hadn't cared which.

The surge of fury set his pulses racing. He took several steps forward without being aware that he had moved at all. After that, it wasn't quite so hard to keep on walking; easier, in fact, than standing still and counting his bruises as they made themselves felt.

His attackers had not left him where he had fallen, after all. He had been dragged around a corner and into a dark side street. There were lights ahead and the sound of traffic.

He paused as another thought came to him and belatedly he checked for his wallet and passport. Still there. He hadn't really believed it had been an ordinary mugging. They had just wanted to get him out of the way . . . while they went after Hope.

The rest of it was coming back now. The hikers had moved swiftly when Hope, the other woman and the child had suddenly reappeared on the far side of Boulevard Roosevelt. The chase had been on again.

Grimmer, this time—the quarry had escaped before—they had followed her. He had followed them, until— They must have spotted him them. Or someone had.

He stumbled forward a few more steps, as though he could run away from the returning memories. There were just a few more of them before he was knocked out of the picture. He didn't want to remember but—

The bridge.

The pursuers had stopped just short of it, watching as the

two women and the child crossed it. It was brightly lit
and they preferred the shadows, he had thought. Now he
wondered if they had been waiting for someone else to
reinforce them. The person, or persons, who were busy
stalking Russ and just about to put him out of the way.

Unsuspecting, he had breathed a sigh of relief as Hope
and her friends reached comparative safety on the far side
of the bridge. Then the trio had stopped. There seemed to
be an argument, then one of the women turned and began
hurrying back across the bridge.

She had been at the halfway point when the men moved
forward to intercept her.

Russ had started forward himself but . . . But that had
been the point at which someone had struck him down. As
he lost consciousness, he had heard the sound of breaking
glass . . . and then those dreadful screams . . .

*Hope!* No, he did not think it had been Hope. He thought
it had been the other woman. But he could not be sure,
would not be sure, until he had found Hope herself.

Where was she now? Where were any of them? Three
persons lost—one irretrievably—in this strange two-tiered
city and he had not the faintest idea where to find them.
Make that four persons—he didn't know where he was
himself.

He had reached a main thoroughfare and gradually recognized it. He had been this way before. Only then he was
paying more attention to the people in front of him than to
his surroundings. They had all turned in this direction and,
yes, there was the bridge just ahead.

He approached it cautiously. It was deserted and dark.
One of the lights was broken. There was no other sign of
drama, past or present. No police activity, no gossiping
crowd; the glass from the broken lamp had not even been
swept away. It crunched underfoot as he went to the parapet
and peered over.

All was dark and silent below, too. No flashing lights, no

movement of police investigating or ambulancemen removing a broken body. He might have dreamt it all, except
for his aching head and the desperate sense of loss and
helplessness.

He had promised to help Hope. Some help he had been!

He was getting dizzy just looking down into the canyon
below. So far, so deep, so easy to lose your balance and—

He pushed himself away from the railing. He was feeling
steadier now and all he wanted was to get off this bridge. If
he kept straight ahead, it would lead him to the railway
station. That must have been where Hope was heading.
Had she ever reached it?

Could *he* reach it? His legs wobbled again. Not far ahead,
he saw a small restaurant, busy now with late diners. It
would make sense to stop there and get something to eat,
while he rested and tried to regain some strength. Then he
could plan his next move. He would be no use to anyone if
he collapsed.

## CHAPTER 13

It was uphill work trying to move Jan-Carl uphill.

There was a delicate balance to be struck between pulling
him along and dislocating his arm. He wasn't helping me
any. He dug in his heels periodically, storming at me in
Swedish. My patience was wearing thin and I raged back
at him in English, occasionally using words I hoped he
wouldn't pick up and repeat in polite company. We weren't
liking each other very well, but I was bigger and stronger—
and winning.

'Come *on!*' He had stopped again. 'Come on, Jan-Carl!
I'm getting fed up with this!'

He let me know how he felt, too, and it was probably just
as well that I didn't speak the language. I was beginning to

understand all those frantic mothers who smacked their kids in the supermarket. Jan-Carl was just one hairsbreadth away from a nasty shock.

Except . . . the poor little wretch had already had the worst shock that life could provide. So had I . . . almost. It wasn't *my* mother who had been murdered.

'*Please*, Jan-Carl.' Sympathy gave me fresh patience. 'Please, don't be difficult. We have to get away from here.' I exerted a firm gentle pressure and he moved forward reluctantly. 'That's a good boy. Just keep moving. Slow and steady wins the race.'

I wished I believed that. I didn't even know what race we were running—or where the finishing line was. Our only chance was to get away completely—out of this country, back to the safety of the States, the North Shore. Home. It seemed so far away tonight that it might be just a pleasant dream I had once had, with no reality at all behind it.

But it *was* real. So was Buck . . . for a little while longer. I felt as young and forlorn as Jan-Carl and longed to be able to swing open the study door and rush in and bury my face against Buck's shoulder and feel his comforting arms and know that all was right with my world.

Only it wasn't. And, for all I knew, Buck might have slipped away from us even as I fought to bring his great-grandson home to him.

This time, it was I who stopped as tears blurred my vision and I could not see the path ahead.

'*Faster Hope?*' Jan-Carl looked up at me, his small hand tightened in mine. '*Faster Hope?*'

*Faster* meant Aunt, I had picked up that much. He wasn't urging me to speed, he was calling my name, trying to comfort me. With his free hand, he reached into a pocket and pulled out a handkerchief. He offered it to me hesitantly, yet with a touch of pride. He was too big a boy to cry, but he understood it if I needed to.

'Thank you, Jan-Carl.' I took it and dabbed at my eyes. 'I'm sorry. I—I—'

He nodded and, from somewhere in the depths of his being, dredged up a small reassuring smile. Then he stepped forward, taking the lead, and we resumed our climb up the hill to the main part of town.

The tears had been unexpected and unintentional, but they had been the best thing I could have done. He was with me now and not against me. The two of us against the unknown enemy.

Or were they really so unknown? I wondered how much Jan-Carl could have told me, if only we spoke the same language.

Still, he was doing very well. I looked down at him with approval. The situation would be worse if he had started crying. It was possible that he was so deep in shock that it would take psychiatric treatment to deal with it, but I'd worry about that later.

It did not occur to me then that I was in a state of shock myself. For one who had led a reasonably sheltered life, I had still encountered a series of shocks during it. All of them delivered in one way or another, by Tad. Not that he would have ever realized it, of course. He had probably never considered any repercussions to the family at all from his initial act. Just as he had not understood that he could be placing Inga and Jan-Carl in danger because of this new mess he had got himself into.

I found my lifelong sympathy for Tad was wearing thin. I began to wonder how well I had ever really known him. He had been so much older that we had effectively lived in different worlds. He had been the big brother I had automatically looked up to, without asking myself if he really deserved such adulation. Just as automatically, I had defended him in his disgrace. Now I was beginning to think that Buck might have been right.

'*Faster Hope*—' Jan-Carl tugged consolingly at my hand. '*Min Pappa kommer att rädda oss.*'

'Will he, indeed?' I asked wryly. I had got Pappa—that was Tad—and *kommer* sounded like come. Was he expecting Tad to come and find us, perhaps help us? If so, I thought with growing annoyance, he still had a lot to learn about his father.

Perhaps I had never really known Tad, either. More to the point, would I know him now? I realized suddenly that, apart from one blurred photograph (had he moved purposely at the last minute?), I had no idea what Tad looked like today. He might have changed enormously over the past years, grown heavy, grown wrinkles, grown a beard. I could pass him in the street and not recognize him— unless he chose to let me.

But Jan-Carl would know him. The thought relaxed me. I was worrying about things that might never happen. It was probably some form of self-protection, to keep me from worrying about the problems that faced me now.

We were still moving uphill, although our pace had slowed. At first, I had tried not to go too fast, so that Jan-Carl's little legs could keep up with me, but I was getting tired myself. These steep hills made me feel as though I were mountain-climbing, and my legs were aching.

'Not much farther—' I was encouraging myself more than Jan-Carl, who could not understand me. We were on pavement more often than not and occasional houses could be glimpsed from along our path. At the top of the incline, a serried row of lights glittered, suggesting civilization or, at least, a main thoroughfare.

'We're almost there,' I promised.

Jan-Carl looked up and followed my gaze. We both quickened our steps towards the bright lights. I wondered if he were afraid of the dark. After this, he might be. So might I.

'Shhh!' He squeezed my hand fearfully. He was right. We

could not tell who might be lurking in the surrounding darkness, waiting . . . and listening.

We moved forward in silence, saving all our energies for the last steep climb to level ground.

When we made it, I was relieved to find that we were on the railway side of the bridge. I knew that I could not have forced myself over one of those bridges again—and it would have been the worst sort of cruelty to make Jan-Carl venture out on one. For good or ill, our course was decided: it was to be the train back to Brussels . . . as Inga had planned.

The street was almost deserted. A woman was walking her dog, a pair of lovers strolled hand-in-hand, but they were all a comfortable distance ahead of us. The dog halted at a lamp-post, the lovers turned a corner. We had the street almost to ourselves.

I halted us at the next lamp-post and used the light to check on our appearance before we went any farther. Jan-Carl was no longer the immaculately dressed child we had started out with. His hands and face were grimy, his jacket streaked with mud and one sock had disappeared into his shoe. I didn't feel a great deal cleaner or better dressed myself.

I took out my own handkerchief and thrust it under his nose. 'Spit!' I commanded.

The gesture was obviously universal and he obeyed without question. I began to feel that we could manage fairly well communicating in pantomime. He winced as I scrubbed at his face and hands, but did not draw away.

When I had finished, he took control of the handkerchief and issued a command of his own.

I spat dutifully and crouched so that he could work on my face. It must have been worse than I thought, for it was some time before he was satisfied. He restored the handkerchief to me and we grinned ruefully at each other, then he replaced his hand in mine.

We set off down the street, looking if not feeling somewhat

better. A couple more turnings took us on to the main street leading down to the station. It also took us past some restaurants. Prior to this, I had not thought much about food; now the fragrant odours assailed me from all sides and turned my knees weak.

Jan-Carl sniffed and slowed his steps. He looked up at me hopefully, apologetically. He felt that he should not be thinking of food, but he was young and healthy—and hungry. I wondered when he had eaten last.

'Hungry?' I asked. We both looked towards the lighted windows, through which we could see tables and customers and waiters darting about with loaded trays.

'Come on.' I led him towards the nearest. 'It won't do anyone any good if we starve ourselves. Wait a minute—' Belated caution caught up with me. 'Let's see what we're getting into first.'

We stopped short of the plate glass window and peered inside. It looked safe enough. Plenty of the locals filled the tables—always a good sign—and no faces I would rather not see.

And one face I had not expected to see again! Look at him—stuffing himself without a care in the world, while Jan-Carl and I had been plunging through the undergrowth not knowing who might be in pursuit. My hero!

'Come on!' I tugged Jan-Carl through the doors. 'He's not getting away with this!'

Dragging a bewildered Jan-Carl in my wake, I stormed up to his table and stood there until he became aware of me.

'Hope!' He pushed back his chair and struggled to his feet—still chewing. 'Thank God! I've been worried sick about you!'

'I notice that didn't put you off your food,' I said sweetly. 'Consider yourself fired!'

'Now wait a minute. You haven't heard my side of the story.'

'I can *see* your side. Don't let us interrupt your meal. We wouldn't want to disturb you.'

'Hold on!' He caught my arm as I started to move away. 'You might at least give me a chance to explain.'

'I'm not interested. Let me go!'

'Excuse me, miss—' A large, burly man rose from an adjoining table. 'Is this man bothering you?'

'He's infuriating me!' I snapped.

'Right!' A massive fist closed over Russ's wrist. 'Just let her go, buddy. We wouldn't want a nasty scene, would we?'

'I don't know how you got into this argument,' Russ said. 'But you can get right out of it again. This is a private dispute.'

'Not the way you're shouting. The whole world's in on the argument. And this girl is an American. I'm not going to stand around and let you bully her.'

'We're all Americans,' Russ snarled.

'*Jag tycker inte om Amerikanare!*' Jan-Carl was in a bad temper himself.

'What did that kid say?'

'I'm nót sure,' Russ said, 'but it sounded like the local equivalent of "Americans, go home!"'

'He's hungry,' I said quickly. 'We came in here to eat.'

'You couldn't prove that by me,' Russ said.

'Miss, this place is crowded, but I'd be very pleased if you'd join me at my table—'

'She'll eat at my table,' Russ said. 'Believe it or not, we're together.'

'I won't believe it unless she tells me. Is that so, miss?'

'Actually, I'm afraid it is. We have our little disagreements, but basically—' I gave him my best smile and a shrug, trying to ease the situation. Furious though I was, I'd still rather stick with the devil I knew.

'Thank you very much, though.' I subsided into the chair Russ held for me. 'You've been very kind.'

'I tried,' he said. 'If this guy gives you any more trouble, well, I'm right here. My name is Jack Kanavski, by the way.'

I nodded and let my smile grow vaguer, then picked up the menu and huddled over it with Jan-Carl.

'Well . . .' Eventually he took the hint. 'Like I said, I'm right here if you need me.'

'She won't,' Russ said decisively. 'The argument is over.' He sat down and shifted his chair so that his back was towards the other table.

It wasn't a bad idea. I edged my own chair round so that the view of—and from—the adjoining table was blocked off. Then I returned my attention to Jan-Carl and the menu. I ran my finger over the *Plat du Jour* and up and down the *A la Carte* listings, indicating that he could have anything he wanted. At the same time, I wondered if he could read the menu.

He solved the problem by waving the menu aside and pointing at Russ's plate.

'I'll have the same, too, I decided. The steak and *frites* looked and smelled delicious. I realized I was faint with hunger. 'Tell the waiter to hurry.'

'How do you want it; rare, medium or well-done?'

'I'll have medium and—' I hadn't the faintest notion whether or not that might be good for a child. 'Jan-Carl had better have his well-done.' That ought to be safe.

Russ ordered and threw in onion soup to start with. I wasn't going to argue. It came quickly and Jan-Carl and I began to eat as though we couldn't remember our last meal. The hot soup began to restore me and some colour came back into Jan-Carl's cheeks.

When the steaks arrived, I cut into mine and watched the pink juice dribble on to my plate. Jan-Carl cut into his and frowned.

He put down his knife and fork, reached over, and very firmly exchanged plates with me.

'I guess he wanted it medium,' I explained as Russ raised his eyebrows. 'It's all right, I don't mind well-done.' I didn't mind anything, so long as I could get some nourishment into me.

'In my family, we were taught to say "Excuse me—" or even to ask permission first.' He studied Jan-Carl thoughtfully. 'What's the matter, cat got your tongue?'

Jan-Carl flicked an uneasy glance across the table, sensing that he was being criticized.

'Let it go,' I said. 'I'll explain later.'

'So you *do* admit there's something to explain?' Russ shifted his thoughtful gaze to me. 'I can hardly wait.'

I ignored him ostentatiously and concentrated on my food. He signalled for coffee. He did have his uses. It was a shame he wasn't more reliable.

'Would you like to hear my side of it?' He might have been reading my mind.

'Oh? Do you have a side?'

'And quite a few bruises. Plus a nasty lump on my head.'

'Really? I'm sorry to hear that.' Perhaps my tone left something to be desired. Did he seriously expect me to get upset over a few bumps and bruises—after what we'd been through?

'I mean,' he said stiffly, 'I was knocked unconscious. Deliberately.'

'But you've survived.' I had a sudden vision of Inga's body hurtling through space; her scream echoed in my ears. I put down my knife and fork; all appetite gone.

'I'm sorry,' he said quickly. 'I tried to help. I was running from the other end of the bridge when someone ambushed me. Did she—?'

'I wasn't able to reach her in time, either.' I glanced at Jan-Carl and lowered my voice. 'Then they started after us. We had to run . . . for our lives.'

'Who were they? What did they want?'

'Shhh!' Jan-Carl had stopped eating. Either he had sensed the subject under discussion or our lowered voices had given us away. He set down his knife and fork with an air of finality. He was blinking hard and would not look up.

'Oh-oh!' Russ caught on at once. He mouthed silently to me: *His mother?*

I nodded. 'I'll tell you later.'

'Right. What do we do now?'

'We're going home. As fast as we can. And he's coming with us.'

'Sounds like a good idea to me. What does he think of it?'

'He'll come.' He had no choice. The poor child was literally alone in the world—except for me. Inga might have left relatives in Sweden, but we were in Luxembourg. Perhaps Jan-Carl had just realized that. No wonder he had lost his appetite.

Jan-Carl suddenly looked directly at me and, wriggling uncomfortably, did a most unconvincing pantomime of washing his hands. He pushed back his chair and headed purposefully for the toilets.

'Go with him, Russ,' I said quickly. 'Keep an eye on him.'

Russ was already on his feet as I spoke. He followed Jan-Carl and I relaxed. But only momentarily. I was now in full view of my would-be friend, Jack. He smiled at me and leaned forward.

I smiled apologetically and fled to the Ladies Room, scooping up Jan-Carl's suitcase and pausing *en route* at the Cashier's Desk to settle our bill so that we could leave as soon as they had finished.

With luck, there might be a back exit and we would not have to pass Jack's table again. Maybe he was just an innocent tourist, honestly trying to help a lady he considered in distress, but I didn't trust anyone right now. The childhood instruction dinned into me—*Don't speak to strangers*—was right and I intended to abide by it.

I hoped it had also been instilled into Jan-Carl, then realized that it didn't matter. No one would be able to understand what he was saying, anyway.

*

'This kid doesn't speak English!' was Russ's aggrieved greeting as they emerged to find me waiting for them.

'I know,' I said, 'but he's awfully good at understanding what you mean. Just try a bit of pantomime.'

'Try?' Russ snorted. 'By this time, I could give Marcel Marceau lessons. How are we going to get him back to the States like this?'

'I'm going to vouch for him,' I said. 'He *is* my nephew.'

'*Is* he?' Russ gave a soundless whistle. 'And now you've got him, you're going home. What about—?' he broke off.

'The child is all that matters now.' I smiled at Jan-Carl, who was watching me warily. 'There's a side exit, we needn't go back through the restaurant. Let's get to the station.'

## CHAPTER 14

With a vague idea of covering our tracks, I bought round-trip tickets to Brussels. Russ winced at the waste of money, but it was my money and I ignored him.

By common consent, we sought the darkest corner of the platform and huddled together waiting for our train. I kept constant watch for any of the figures I had learned to recognize and dread, but they did not appear. None of the other travellers filtering out on to the platform seemed to have any interest in us. I hoped it was true.

The outraged spinster suddenly whooped in the distance and the train came thundering towards the station, slowing at the last moment. We hung back as the waiting passengers crowded forward.

My spirits began to lighten at the prospect of immediate escape. It was a nice country—if you were a *bona fide* tourist —but I would be glad to leave the Grand Duchy well behind me.

'The coast looks clear,' Russ said. 'Let's go!'

A final look over my shoulder showed no pursuers making a last-minute dash along the platform to catch up with us. Even so, I did not feel comfortable until I heard the doors slam, the whistles blow, and saw the station slowly begin to slide past.

Jan-Carl leaned back against the seat and gave an involuntary sigh of relief. He, too, had been feeling the strain.

'So, now we are three.' Russ did not seem quite so relieved. 'Would you mind telling me how you propose to smuggle this kid past the international Immigration barriers?'

'It's all right.' I fished in my shoulder-bag. 'I have his passport.' I surfaced, waving it triumphantly. 'See?'

'A Swedish passport,' Russ said thoughtfully, reaching for it.

'That's right.' I flipped it open as I passed it to him. 'And perfectly in order—' I broke off, feeling as though I had just received a blow in the solar plexus.

Inga, her arm around Jan-Carl, smiled into the camera. It was a mother-and-child passport.

'*Mamma!*' Jan-Carl saw the photo and his precarious passivity shattered. '*Mamma!*' He lunged to snatch at the passport. '*Mamma!*' Tears exploded from him.

'Oh, Jan-Carl, Jan-Carl!' I gathered him into my arms, my own tears flowing freely. 'Poor baby! I'm sorry, I'm so sorry.'

Russ retrieved the passport as it slid to the floor between us. To his credit, he didn't try to be soothing. He frowned tactfully out of the window until we had regained control and dried our eyes.

Then, exhausted, Jan-Carl leaned against me and fell asleep. I envied him. I was equally exhausted, but sleep was beyond me. Every click of the wheels was like the tick of a clock, inexorably marking the passage of time, the dwindling of the hours allotted to us. To Buck.

Outside, the night was black and moonless. An occasional light gleamed in the distance. We must be passing through the forests again. I realized how carefree, comparatively speaking, I had been on the journey to Luxembourg; now I felt that I carried the weight of the world on my shoulders.

'He's asleep,' Russ said softly. 'Can we talk?'

'I suppose so.' I shifted to a slightly more comfortable position, but Jan-Carl did not stir. 'Poor baby, he's dead to the world.'

'He's not the only one,' Russ said. 'Whoever they are, those people are playing for keeps.'

'Poor Inga.' Part of my mind had been considering that problem. 'As soon as we get back, I'll have money and instructions cabled to the Luxembourg authorities. The bod—*She* ought to be sent back to Sweden for burial—'

I stopped. Was that what Tad would want? Or should she be interred in the North Shore plot with the rest of the family?

With Buck . . . any time now.

'What's the matter?' Russ asked. 'Just realized that perhaps the Bradstone money can't sort out everything?'

'Oh, don't!' This was no time for him to start sniping at me. 'You don't understand. I'm so confused.'

'Poor kid, I guess you are.' He was sympathetic again. 'It's a hard cold world out there, isn't it? Not the sort of thing you're accustomed to, at all.'

'I was born into money,' I said. 'Is that my fault? It hasn't done much towards keeping anything but the wolf from my door, has it? Everything else seems to be lining up to get at me!'

'Money can't buy happiness but, as they say, it sure can make misery comfortable.'

'Can it?' Suddenly, I didn't like him very much. 'Do you really think I've had such clear sailing all the way?'

'No.' He was chastened. 'No, I guess you've had your problems.' In a sudden non-sequitur, he added, 'And the kid doesn't even speak English.'

'Tad must have been very bitter.' There was no point in

pretending this wasn't what we were talking about. 'You can't blame him, when you think of all he went through.'

'I'm beginning to see,' Russ said grimly, 'that he put the rest of you through quite a lot, too. And still is.'

'That's not his fault.' Old habits die hard—I was back to defending Tad again.

'Isn't it? You're not going to try to tell me that it was yours? Or anyone else in your family—?'

'Well, perhaps—' It pained me to admit it. 'Perhaps Buck pushed him too hard. Buck had such great expectations—'

'A serious mistake. As Dickens pointed out.'

'Oh, stop it! You don't know anything about it—except what you must have read in the papers. And that was the worst of it. You don't know what we went through— hounded by those terrible reporters! Flashbulbs exploding in our faces every time we tried to leave the house . . . newspapers printing rumours, speculations—and just plain lies . . .'

'Mamma?' I had leaned forward in my fury and Jan-Carl's head had slipped off my shoulder and hit the back of the seat, jolting him into wakefulness. 'Mamma?'

'Now see what you've done!' I cradled Jan-Carl in my arms, stroking his head, trying to will him back to sleep. 'It's all right, Jan-Carl, it's all right.'

It was not all right. I was not Mamma. Jan-Carl stiffened, memory obviously returning. He gave a long, shuddering sigh and burrowed his head into my shoulder, trying to retreat into the merciful oblivion where the world was safe and happy again.

'I'm sorry.' Russ appeared shaken. 'I hadn't realized you'd had such a tough time. I guess you don't like reporters very—' He broke off, looking at me almost pleadingly.

'*Like* them? You don't know how much I despise them! You couldn't know what they're like.' I forgave him. 'No one could. Normal people wouldn't believe the way they persecuted us—and all in the sacred name of the Public's

Right to Know. The reporters' right to get their names in a rotten by-line, they mean. I hated them all! I still do!'

'I'm sorry,' he said again, almost abject in the apology.

'Forget it.' I shrugged the shoulder Jan-Carl wasn't lying against. 'But remember that, having been mixed up in a Nine-Days'-Wonder once, I'm not anxious to have it happen again. You can sneer at our money, but we'll pay anything for privacy. It's worth it.'

'I can understand why you value it.' He made the admission almost grudgingly. 'Look—' he stood up abruptly—'I think I'll take a look through the train—just to make sure none of our chums are aboard. I'll say I'm looking for the Buffet Car if anyone asks. In case I actually find it, would you like a cup of coffee? And what about Jan-Carl?'

'Hot chocolate for him,' I decided. 'For me, too, in fact. If he doesn't wake up, then I can drink his.'

'Good thinking.' He sketched a salute and departed.

I wished I could go with him; I didn't want to sit here and wait for him to report back to me.

But Jan-Carl anchored me here. I fought against resentment. Jan-Carl was the reason I was here. If it hadn't been for him, I wouldn't have come over here at all. If it hadn't been for Inga's unreasonableness—my resentment veered in another direction—I wouldn't have needed to come. She should have brought him to New England herself.

She had paid for that mistake.

And left me holding the baby—although not quite in the ·way she had intended. Or had she known just how desperate her danger was? She had given me their joint passport— had she suspected she would not need it again. Without a passport, she would not have been able to cross any major frontiers.

Or would she? I looked out at the apparently limitless forest we were crossing. There must be many uncharted ways across borders. There was only one Berlin Wall; most countries did not try to fence off their entire area. They had open borders, relying on checkpoints at highways, ports and airports.

Anyway, how did I know that Inga didn't have another passport—or two, or three? Tad had evidently been playing with some very strange companions over the past years; he would have had access to all sorts of documentation and credentials—for a price.

I leaned my head back against the seat as my weary brain registered afresh that it was too late to worry about anything Inga might have planned.

I ought to get some sleep. I closed my eyes but they sprang open again. I was too mistrustful to sleep. Jan-Carl stirred against my shoulder and I wondered what nightmares might be haunting him. And whether they were lying in wait for me, too.

It seemed hours before Russ returned. I had time to imagine him ambushed, as Inga had been, and hurled from the train down into the black depths of the Ardennes, to die there, perhaps in the company of some skeleton left over from the War before last.

Or perhaps he wasn't coming back. Perhaps he was one of *Them*—whoever *They* were.

No! My imagination boggled at that. Russ had accompanied me all the way from Boston on the same plane. And Buck was a better judge of men than that; he would not have entrusted me to anyone who was not totally loyal —and ambitious.

The lights in the carriage dimmed. Other passengers throughout the length of the train would be relaxing and trying to get some sleep, especially those booked through to the final terminus. This train went all the way to the Belgian coast, to connect with the night ferry to England. I had already noticed, with a certain amount of wistful envy, that some luggage bore tags reading 'Ostende–Victoria'. How nice to be heading for a vacation with no worries and able to look forward to arriving at your destination.

*Journeys end in lovers' meetings.* Not this one. Not that kind of love. The best I could hope for was that Buck would still be waiting for us, that we would have him for a while longer. And I wondered if I would dare tell him the truth about this journey, if he would be strong enough to hear it.

On the other hand, I didn't actually have a choice about what I'd tell him. It was going to take a platoon of Bradstone Enterprises's best legal talent to sort out the International mess I had left behind me. Buck was going to have to know.

Also, Russ would probably report to him as soon as we reached home. It was what he was being paid for, after all.

Where was he? He had been gone long enough to sketch every last passenger aboard the train.

Jan-Carl whimpered in his sleep and I patted his shoulder. Poor baby, he was too young to deal with the horror of what he had seen. I could barely deal with it myself and I tried not to think about the repercussions. I wondered whether the authorities would make me return to give evidence or whether they would be content with the deposition our lawyers would transmit to them. And then there was the question of shipping Inga's body home—to whichever home we decided upon . . .

'Why don't you try to sleep?' Russ was back, frowning down at me.

'Oh!' I jumped and spoke crossly to cover it. 'You're back at last, are you? I was beginning to think the trolls had got you.'

'Trolls are Scandinavian,' he said. 'The Luxembourg variation is the *Tollchen*, a militant teetotaller dedicated to making men give up drinking. Legend has it, he was a watchman who chased drunkards, hurling barrels at them and howling unearthly animal cries. But he lurks around the Hesperage area and I hope he isn't on the train—' Russ pulled a small flask out of his pocket—'because I managed to get this by bribery and corruption of one of the train staff. I thought we could both use something stronger than hot chocolate.'

'I think you're right.' I watched as a strange bulge in his jacket pocket turned into two plastic glasses, complete with ice. Something else was puzzling me now.

'You seem to know a lot—including local legends. Are you sure you're quite the stranger to these parts you've been pretending to be?'

'I never claimed to be a stranger, you just assumed that. In fact, I've kicked around quite a bit of the world—including Europe.' He poured the drink quickly and handed it to me. 'I know some places better than others, but I've picked up a bit about most countries.'

'How convenient.' Yet it figured. Buck would not have sent an absolute tyro to watch over me.

'I wouldn't be much use to you, otherwise, would I?'

'I suppose not.' I sipped the drink and yawned. For a moment, suspicion flared, then I decided it was unlikely he had added anything to the drink; he wouldn't have needed to. I was knocked out enough already. I had to trust him and I was so tired . . .

'That's right . . .' His voice came from a long distance away. 'Get some sleep.'

I didn't sleep well, but I slept. Always, however, I was aware of Russ sitting in the seat opposite me and the slowing and stopping of the train at stations along the way. I was aware, too, of the leaden weight of Jan-Carl's body slumped against mine. Occasionally, I struggled back to enough wakefulness to look at my watch. We hadn't much farther to go.

When the first signs for BRUXELLES-NORD slid past outside, I sat up and eased Jan-Carl away from me.

'Don't wake him yet,' Russ said. 'Let's take a look at the lie of the land first.'

'You don't think—' I broke off. They could easily have beaten us to Brussels if they had flown. If they had gone directly to the airport as soon as they had lost us in Luxembourg, they could be waiting for us here. Perhaps outside, perhaps at the airport, perhaps at the *Poisson d'Or*, where they had found me first. Suddenly, Brussels seemed as fraught with potential danger as Luxembourg had been.

Russ peered intently out of the window, scrutinizing the waiting passengers. I shrank back against the seat, hoping I could not be seen.

The platform outside was crowded with backpackers, some in shorts, some in jeans, some tilting forward to counterbalance the weight of their equipment, others bending to pick up the packs and struggle into them. There was an army of them; their faces shadowed and hidden. Anyone could have infiltrated their ranks.

'I don't know—' Russ turned to me, frowning. 'Want to risk it?'

Even as he spoke, two of the backpackers stepped back from the crowd and turned their heads to scan the lighted windows of the train. They might be innocent passengers, just waiting for the next train. They might not. A European railway station with trains going to different destinations from the same platform, was an ideal spot for a stakeout. Watchers could wait there for any length of time, unnoticed. The constant flow of passengers would ensure that no one else was on the platform long enough to realize that they were lurking there for a purpose.

'I don't know . . .' I echoed. 'What do you think?'

'I don't like it,' he said. 'But, if you want to, we'll make a run for it.'

'There are those long flights of stairs—and we'd have to carry Jan-Carl . . .' I realized Russ was no more anxious than I was to leave the comparative safety of the busy train and try to cross a strange city in the dead of night. We didn't know who might be out there. 'What's the alternative?'

'We could stay on the train,' he suggested. 'Pay the supplementary fare and go straight through to Ostende and catch the ferry. We'd be in England in the morning. It would be just as easy to catch a flight from there. Perhaps easier.'

'All right.' Relief swept over me. If we did that, we would be surrounded by lights and people all the way—and we would land where everyone spoke English. I listened to the babble of voices around us and realized I was longing to hear casual conversations in English again. 'Let's do that.'

'Right you are.' He beamed at me approvingly. 'We don't even know if we could connect with a flight from Brussels at this hour, but we ought to have our choice of flights from England tomorrow.'

Outside, whistles were blowing. The train was not going to linger; it had other stations to stop at before it connected with the night ferry. The newly-boarded passengers struggled along the aisles, shouting to each other and crashing their backpacks against the seats. There seemed to be an awful lot of them.

'I hope there are enough seats for them all.' I meant I hoped we wouldn't have to share our seat space with anyone. Russ had piled our cases on the seat beside him to discourage any such idea. 'I never expected such a late train to be so crowded.'

'Of course, it's Friday! I'd lost track . . .' Russ's face cleared. 'That explains it. They'll be on some sort of cheap Weekend in London excursion. They can nap on board the ferry and save the cost of a night in a hotel.'

The train slid away from the station, leaving shadowed figures still staring after it.

'Then perhaps—' I had a sudden doubt. 'Perhaps those other people are just weekenders heading for Paris or Amsterdam.'

'Perhaps,' he said, 'but we can't be sure, can we?'

## CHAPTER 15

He hated to wake her, but the lights of Ostende were coming into view in the distance. The other passengers were stirring, yawning, pulling down luggage from overhead racks, struggling into sweaters and jackets, talking to each other in gradually rising voices.

'Hope—' He caught her wrist and shook it gently. 'We're nearly there. Wake up.'

She sighed and tried to pull away, resisting, wanting to remain in the shelter of sleep. However, Jan-Carl's eyelids flew open and he stared around blankly, awake but recognizing nothing of his surroundings. After a moment, pain replaced the blank look in his eyes. Memory had returned.

'I'm sorry,' Russ said, 'but we're nearly at the ferry . . . the boat . . . the ship . . .' He gave up and gestured to the window.

Jan-Carl looked out and nodded comprehension, but now there was sadness as well as pain in his eyes. Russ remembered that Stockholm was on the water. The Venice of the North, it was called, with commuter ferries plentiful as gondolas on dozens of routes between the network of islands and the city. Probably the last time Jan-Carl had been on a ferry had been with his mother.

'What is it?' Hope sprang to life, frightened.

'It's all right. We're coming into Ostende. I wanted to talk to you before we go through Immigration—'

'You think there'll be trouble?'

'There shouldn't be, but I've been thinking.' He could not help a sideways glance at Jan-Carl. 'It might be better if you went through on Inga's passport. That would save explanations as to why we're travelling with a child who has half a passport. You still have that yellow wig, haven't you?'

'In my bag, but it's in dreadful shape.'

'That doesn't matter. Everyone knows you're just off the boat train and not out of a bandbox. They're used to it.'

'I suppose so.' Automatically, she smoothed her hair, then began searching through her holdall for the wig.

'Also . . .' He hesitated.

'Yes?' She looked up suspiciously, catching the hesitation.

'Your name.' He had to remind her. 'It might be recognized. Especially if . . . anything has happened. You'll be inconspicuous if you use the passport with a different name.'

'Different name?' He'd thought she hadn't noticed it. She had just got a glimpse of the passport before the boy had broken up. 'Isn't it Bradstone? She was my brother's wife.'

'Maybe she was, but the passport says Swenson.'

'Her maiden name. But . . . I don't understand.'

'Never mind, just be grateful.' The picture was becoming clearer all the time. It was not unusual for people in certain circles to have more than one passport under more than one name—and Thaddeus Bradstone had travelled a great distance from the privileged environment of his youth. 'It means you can slide through Immigration without arousing comment.'

'In case anything . . .' She picked up his earlier comment and threw it back at him. 'Anything has happened . . . to Buck. In case the Bradstone name is in the news . . . again.'

'That's right.' This was no time for sympathy. 'In which case, we'll find out soon enough. Right now, you'd better get along to the toilet. You'll attract less attention if you get into the wig in there.'

Jan-Carl tensed as Hope left her seat.

'It's okay, she'll be right back,' Russ said. There was no response and he remembered that the child did not speak

English. 'Uh—she's just gone—' He pantomimed washing his hands, combing his hair, powdering his nose. 'She'll be right back.' He tapped his watch.

He might as well have spared his efforts. The boy had not even glanced at him; all his worried concentration was given to the door through which Hope had disappeared. He seemed to hold his breath until the door opened and Hope reappeared, then he slumped back against the seat, limp with relief.

'I'm glad you were fast,' Russ told her. 'We might have had quite a problem on our hands, otherwise.'

The train was slowing to a halt in the brightly lit station, already doors were clattering open and the first feet hit the ground as the train stopped. There was a mass charge towards the Customs Hall by those eager to be first aboard the ferry.

The aisle of their carriage was blocked by departing passengers laden with luggage, unwittingly turning their backpacks into dangerous blunt instruments.

'Plenty of time.' Russ was deliberately soothing as both Hope and Jan-Carl wriggled with impatience. 'The ferry won't leave until everyone is aboard.'

He leaned back casually, keeping watch from the window. Just checking. They might possibly have missed seeing old acquaintances board the train at Brussels, or—and this was a more disquieting thought—another set of followers might already have been aboard when the train pulled in at Luxembourg. For an outfit with sufficient resources, it was not unknown for teams to work in relays.

'You think they may be—' He hadn't fooled Hope; she had noticed his careful scrutiny of the passing throng. 'You think they're out there?'

'I think we have to bear the possibility in mind.' He sent her a brief, encouraging smile. 'That's why I'd prefer to be among the last to leave the train.'

'I see.' Uneasily, she rubbed a circle clear on the window

and joined him in the watch, but there was nothing—no one—to see.

When their carriage had cleared, the crowd outside had already thinned. Thankful that their luggage was minimal, Russ took charge of Jan-Carl's suitcase and herded them out of the train and across to the Customs Hall where the lines waiting to pass the Immigration Officers were dwindling rapidly. The Officers were expert at processing the ferry passengers at top speed.

At this hour, some of the passengers were almost sleep-walking. Russ was relieved to see that there were other children for the 2.00 a.m. ferry; he had been afraid that Jan-Carl would stand out and draw attention to them. However, they looked just like any other family party.

The formalities were quickly concluded and they went through the doors on the far side of the room and out on to the dock. The ferry loomed above them, ablaze with light from stem to stern.

Jan-Carl took one quick look at it, then averted his eyes. He stared fixedly at the ground as they walked to the gangplank. A ferry brought back memories of Sweden and his parents—his mother.

Since he didn't understand English, there was no use even trying to say anything that might be of comfort. It was tough on the kid, but he was going to have to fight this through on his own. At least, he knew that he was not completely on his own. He was clinging so tightly to Hope's hand that his knuckles were white. She'd be lucky if he didn't cut off her circulation.

As soon as they were aboard, Russ herded them towards the cafeteria. There was nothing like a bit of grub to save a situation. Also, all the reclining sleep-seats would have been taken by the firstcomers, so the best chance of sitting down all the way across would be at one of the tables. A judicious spacing-out of food and drink would ensure that they could legitimately occupy a table for the entire journey.

Two Arab women, swathed in black robes, faces concealed behind black *yashmaks*, pushed past them abruptly, sending them staggering.

'You don't have to push children around!' Hope snarled after the women, steadying Jan-Carl.

'They don't care about the kiddies,' an aggrieved English voice said behind them. 'Bloody Arab bints can't wait to get to Harrod's and start their shoplifting!'

There was a sudden choking sound from Jan-Carl. Russ glanced down anxiously, half-fearing the long overdue emotional reaction had arrived, and was just in time to see Jan-Carl hastily covering his mouth. But not hastily enough. Russ had caught him.

For the first time since he had met him, Jan-Carl was laughing.

Fortunately, they were all good sailors; they needed to be. The Channel was at its most virulent and was taking its toll of the ferry passengers. The cafeteria was turning out to be not such a good idea, after all. The cooking smells wafting from the galley behind the display counter and the sight of all that food was having a deleterious effect on some of the customers. Several had dashed abruptly for the door, a couple of them hadn't quite made it. Another, far more unpleasant, smell was beginning to pervade the dining area.

With a strangled moan, a young woman at a nearby table hurled herself lengthwise along the wall seat and announced that she'd rather be dead. A thoughtful man with a pale green face sat holding an open paper bag in readiness just below his chin. The ship bounced a couple of times and more people rose quickly and moved towards the doors.

Russ decided that he did not trust the pensive look on Jan-Carl's face, nor the faintly self-pitying expression that was beginning to shadow Hope's face. Distraction was called for.

'Come on.' Russ got up. 'Let's get out of here.'

'Where can we go?' Hope looked at him bleakly. 'It won't stop moving, no matter where we go.'

'We're going to the Duty-Free Shop,' he said firmly. 'You know what they say: when the going gets tough, the tough go shopping.'

'I don't think I'm that tough.' Hope hung back. 'I just don't want to move at all.'

'We'll go along the open deck,' Russ coaxed. 'A breath of fresh air will do us all good.'

'Nothing except land is going to do me any good!'

'Help her up, Jan-Carl,' Russ ordered.

Jan-Carl looked up with an expectant expression, recognizing his name and waiting for the pantomime. Not realizing that he'd given himself away earlier, he was still pretending that he didn't understand English.

Russ sighed and gestured towards Hope, making a lifting motion. Jan-Carl's face cleared; he put his arm around Hope's waist and tried to heave her to her feet.

'On your head be it,' she told Russ.

'Atta gal, you're doing fine.' He took her arm and got her through the door just before the man with the sad green face had his foreboding come true.

Out on deck, the air was clear and crisp. The lights of the port were barely to be seen, the phosphorescent wake of the ship charted their progress. Soon, the lights of Dover would begin to gleam in the distance. A ship was rarely out of sight of land crossing the English Channel.

'The stars are bright tonight,' Russ murmured, steering his charges along the deck.

Jan-Carl glanced upwards automatically; poor kid, he was exhausted and emotionally drained, his reflexes no longer under such good control. Belatedly, he transferred his gaze to the whitecaps lashing against the hull, but he glanced swiftly and guiltily at Russ to see if his lapse had been noticed.

'Here we are.' Russ swung open the door marked by the

symbol for the Duty-Free Shop and arrow pointing the way.
He steadfastly ignored Jan-Carl, who relaxed imperceptibly.

The Duty-Free Shop opened off a clearing at the
end of the passageway, its glass wall blazoned with
posters illustrating the cut-rate delights within. Liquor,
tobacco and perfumes featured largely, but there were
also chocolates, toys and souvenir items. Jan-Carl's expression grew wistful.

Russ nudged Hope and indicated Jan-Carl.

'Do you have any money, Jan-Carl?' Hope asked softly,
burrowing in her shoulder-bag.

Jan-Carl watched her with bright interest.

'Here.' She offered him a couple of Belgian banknotes.
'Go on—take them. We can't use them once we get off the
ship. Oh—' she glanced despairingly at Russ—'how do I
pantomime all that?'

'Don't bother,' Russ said drily. 'I think he's getting the
general idea.'

'*Tak, Faster Hope.*' Jan-Carl took the money, his gaze
already travelling to the display of chocolates, which was
partially blocked from view by the bulky black-robed Arab
women. Undaunted, Jan-Carl sidled nearer to it.

'Stay with us, Jan-Carl,' Hope called, but he was not even
looking back.

'He'll be all right. I'll keep an eye on him,' Russ promised
rashly. 'You go and get a few souvenirs. You know you're
longing to.'

'Well, I could do with something for Everett and Vilma.
And perhaps something extra for—I wish he wouldn't do
that!'

Jan-Carl had pushed between the Arab women and was
almost lost to sight, hidden by their billowing robes.

'Don't worry, they like children. He isn't going to start
an International incident.'

'I couldn't face another one.' She gave a wan smile.
'Aren't you going to do any shopping?'

'Can't afford it. I'm down to my last few centimes—and I don't have a rich aunt.'

'I can take a hint.' She reached for her purse again.

'No.' He stopped her. 'You're already paying all the fares and there's still tomorrow's flight. I was only kidding.'

'You're sure? I still have plenty left. If you're feeling awkward about it, we can always see that it's deducted from your next salary cheque.'

'That's a thought.' He grinned suddenly. 'Why not make it a bonus, instead? You can get me a bottle of the most expensive Scotch—it will make us look like the rest of the tourists when we go through Customs at Dover.'

'All right.' She began to turn away, then stopped. 'Where's Jan-Carl?'

'Buying chocolate—' But the chocolate counter was deserted. 'Perhaps he's gone back on deck.'

'Gone!' Her voice rose as she fought hysteria. 'He's gone!'

Russ was out of the door ahead of her. At the far end of the deck, he saw a flutter of dark draperies in the shadows and—

'JAN-CARL!' He raced towards the boy. 'JAN-CARL!'

Jan-Carl hesitated. Beside him, the draperies fluttered again and whisked away. Jan-Carl turned to follow, but it was too late. Russ had him tightly by the arm.

'Jan-Carl! Oh, you frightened me!' Hope was just a moment behind Russ. She caught Jan-Carl's other arm. 'What were you doing? Where were you going with those awful women?'

Jan-Carl looked at them both with bright-eyed incomprehension and shrugged. What a pity he couldn't understand a word they were saying.

From somewhere ahead and off to one side, there was a loud splash. Someone throwing rubbish overboard. Probably.

'Let's get inside!' Hope shuddered. 'I don't like it out here. And you, Jan-Carl, you stay right here beside me!'

She gestured fiercely to him and to a spot impossibly close
to her. 'Every minute! You understand?'

He nodded and grasped her skirt like a small child, his
eyes dancing, his lips fighting back a smile. There was no
mistake; he was mocking her.

'Come on.' Resisting a strong urge to give Jan-Carl a
good clip across the ear, Russ herded them back inside.

'Now what?' Hope looked at him.

'Now I suggest we finish our shopping, then Jan-Carl can
play the fruit machines, if he wants to—but we don't let
him out of our sight again.'

The sky had turned a paler grey and seagulls wheeled above
the ship, crying their cat-calls as they ushered the ferry
into the harbour. The sea was as grey as the sky and
the streetlamps along the quay were still dimly glowing.
Passengers lined the railings, watching the shore come
closer. The first announcement came over the Tannoy for
all car drivers to return to their vehicles. Impatient foot
passengers, clutching their duty-frees, were already crowding down the staircase to mill about in the lobby where the
gangway would be set up.

Jan-Carl was restless and impatient, too. He jittered
about, casting longing glances towards the stairs, tugging
hopefully at Hope's hand. She looked towards Russ.

'There's no hurry,' he said. 'Let the rowdies get off first,
you don't want to get caught up in all that pushing and
shoving. The train will wait—that's what it's there for.'

'The train may wait, but all the seats will be taken.'

Jan-Carl tugged at her hand again as though endorsing
this view.

'In that case, we go into a first class compartment. They're
never full.'

'We don't have first class tickets. We might get into
trouble. We don't want anything that will delay us now.'

'There won't be any difficulty. When the conductor comes

through, we simply tell him we want to pay the supplement. He'll charge us the difference between our ticket and the first class ticket. It will only be a few pounds and it will be worth it. Er . . . you said you had plenty of money.'

'Yes . . .' she said doubtfully, 'but it's in dollars, not pounds. I should have changed some currency on the ferry but—' she glanced at Jan-Carl—'I got distracted.'

'And it's too late now. The bank on board has closed.' Russ pulled out his wallet and Hope burrowed in her shoulder-bag to produce her change purse. They compared their small hoards of crumpled foreign banknotes.

'Do you think they'll take Belgian francs on the train?' Hope asked.

'They might be preferable to dollars—or they might not.' Russ tried to count the bills. 'It might be better to use dollars —we—*you* have more of them. If we get a sympathetic conductor, we might get away with it.'

Jan-Carl had been following the exchange with bright-eyed interest, but a blank expression. The display of currency and the anxious conference was international, however. Jan-Carl reached into his own pocket and pulled out a crumpled wad of blue and brown notes. Helpfully, he offered them to Hope.

'Jan-Carl, thank you, dear.' She took them automatically, glanced at them and stiffened. 'Where did you get this? This is English money—and so much of it! Where did you get it?'

Jan-Carl looked at her blankly and smiled.

'Perhaps he got his change in English money when he bought his chocolate,' Russ suggested.

'He couldn't have! I didn't give him anything near this much.' She counted it and looked up at Russ in consternation. 'There's fifty pounds here!'

'Well,' Russ said philosophically, 'that will pay for our supplement, with plenty left over for breakfast.'

'But where did he get it? Did you have it all along?' she

asked Jan-Carl. 'Did—did your mother give it to you?'

'Mamma . . .' Jan-Carl said wistfully. 'Mamma . . .' His face clouded over, tears were suddenly perilously close.

'Oh Lord,' Russ said. 'Let it go. Here, give me the money. 'We'll worry about where it came from later.'

'You weren't in the States long, sir.' The English Immigration Officer inspecting Russ's passport picked up the immediate turn-around shown by the Boston entry and exit stamps. His tone was carefully neutral, but his eyes were alert.

'No, it was literally a flying visit.' Russ was thankful that the date stamp did not also carry a time notation. It was just possible that he could have been in Boston for twenty-two or twenty-three hours. There was no evidence to the contrary.

'Mmm . . .' The officer continued to study the passport thoughtfully. Russ felt his face grow warm and a film of perspiration break out on his forehead. The other passengers were streaming past the Immigration Desks on either side of his, their progress marked by the thump of stamp on ink-pad and passport. Even the two Arab women surged through without let or hindrance.

'Travel quite a bit, don't you, sir?' His manner suggested that the only possible reason could be the collecting of shipments of heroin or cocaine, one of which was probably being trans-shipped to England from the Continent at this minute.

'A fair bit, yes.' Russ watched hopefully, but the official showed no sign of reaching for his visa stamp.

'Mmm . . .' He riffled through the passport, looking at the other visas stamped on the crowded pages. At any moment, he was going to whistle up the sniffer dogs and the strip-search team. Possibly even a medic or two who could arrange a fluoroscope examination; with so little luggage, the tiny plastic bags must have been swallowed. 'Quite a bit of it in the Third World Countries, too.'

Russ cursed the fact that he was not in a Third World country right now, where a discreet wad of bills passed under the counter would ensure his immediate release.

Hope was already on the other side of the barrier, staring in his direction, curious about the delay but obviously not quite daring to come and inquire about it. Having got through safely with Jan-Carl, she was not going to risk having something go wrong now. If they delayed him for a body search, he knew that she would abandon him.

He sent Hope what was meant to be a reassuring smile and noticed with alarm that she was edging nearer. If she came much closer, she would be within earshot.

'Actually, I'm a reporter—a journalist—' Russ brought out his press credentials and brandished them over the passport. 'A newsman. I've been on a series of Third World assignments. I had just returned to the Boston Office—' he stretched the truth considerably—'when word came through that another story was breaking. One with local connections, nothing of any international interest—' Just in case the officer might want to know more about it.

'I was right there, with my bag still packed and my passport in good working order, so I got the new assignment. It's finished now and I'm on my way home to write the story. If I can catch the boat train,' he said plaintively, 'I can get to the airport and be on the first plane out.'

'Mmm . . .' The officer checked the Aliens control card Russ had filled out on board the ferry. Fortunately, Hope had been uninterested and he had played safe, entering 'Reporter' in the box for Occupation.

'Yes, well . . .' The visa stamp hit the ink pad and then Russ's passport. 'Have a good flight.'

## CHAPTER 16

As soon as we were comfortably settled, all by ourselves in a first class compartment, I stopped resisting the compulsion to count my money and see how much I had left. I was pleasantly surprised by the total, but disturbed by the way Jan-Carl's bright eyes watched every bill as I counted it.

Where *had* he got all that English currency he had handed over so happily? He hadn't been out of our sight for five minutes.

Uneasily, I reviewed those minutes again. Jan-Carl had gone—I must admit—*pushing* into that crowd in front of the candy counter. I also had to admit that I could see Jan-Carl for a lot longer than I could actually see his hands.

Had he merely been jostling people and pushing them aside—or had be been dipping into someone's pocket?

I could not even feel guilty about speculating as to whether my nephew was a burgeoning pickpocket—those eager blue eyes had watched too avidly as I replaced my money in my shoulder-bag. He knew just which corner it was stowed in. When I went to look for it again, would some—or all—of it be missing?

On the other hand, I tried to be charitable, perhaps he had found the money. Some returning English holidaymaker might have dropped it and walked on, unknowing. Jan-Carl had come along later, spotted it, ducked down quickly to pick it up and . . . But then why hadn't he given it to us right away so that we could turn it in to the Purser's office?

*Finders, keepers; losers, weepers.* Tad had always laughed when he'd snatched up some find from the street. Was that what Jan-Carl had been taught? I knew so little about him. I had never dreamed that some of the things I might learn would not be pleasant.

Jan-Carl curled up in the window seat opposite me and began unwrapping a bar of chocolate, totally absorbed and unconcerned. Who was he, this foreign child I was taking back to a home he had never known? How much, apart from English, did he have to learn—and unlearn?

And what about those Arab women? Where had he been going with them? What did they want? What had they promised him? And how had they managed to understand each other, anyway?

That was something else I did not want to think about right now. In fact, I was getting as good as Scarlett O'Hara with all the things I was going to think about tomorrow.

But tomorrow, I'd be home.

The thought only cheered me for a moment. Would Buck still be there waiting for me? Yet another thing I didn't want to think about.

Jan-Carl looked up and gave me a dazzling smile. Remembering his manners, he offered the chocolate bar to me, and then to Russ.

We both refused. Undoubtedly, for different reasons. Had Jan-Carl had time to buy that chocolate bar, or had someone given it to him? Or had he snatched it and hurried off, hiding himself in the black folds of the Arab robes? Perhaps the women had not even realized what had happened or that he was using them as a cover.

But what about that splash I had heard just after we got Jan-Carl away from them?

Oh, what a conversation we were going to have just as soon as Jan-Carl learned enough English!

'Here comes the conductor,' Russ said. 'I'll do the talking. You just smile and look exhausted.'

I wasn't going to argue. I wasn't going to do anything else, either. I leaned back against the seat and closed my eyes. First class or not, it wasn't as comfortable as the European train, nor as smooth, but I was too tired to care. The conductor and Russ exchanged several merry remarks and I couldn't understand one word the conductor said. Who says we speak the same language?

I let my eyes open again as the compartment door slammed shut behind the conductor and was in time to see Russ putting the remaining pounds away in his wallet. Jan-Carl was watching, too. Of course, it was his money . . . wherever he had got it.

Outside, the tiny houses and long neat back yards streeled past. They looked about the same from both sides of the train.

'There doesn't seem to be a wrong side of the tracks in this country,' I remarked casually. 'There seems to be no difference at all.'

'Leave it to you to think of that!'

'What do you mean?' Why was he so affronted? Had he come from the wrong side of the tracks himself?

'There are places in this world so poverty-stricken that they don't even know what tracks are. Have you ever thought of that?'

'Not recently.' He was over-reacting to an innocent remark, but I found I was ready for a fight myself. 'Why should I? I've had a few other things on my mind.'

'Yes . . .' To my disappointment, he caved in. 'Yes, I guess you have.' He glanced at Jan-Carl. 'And more to come.'

'What is that supposed to mean?' The sneaky sideways look at Jan-Carl annoyed me. Was Russ hinting that he knew where the money had come from? Jan-Carl sat there placidly minding his own business, cheeks puffed out like a chipmunk's with chocolate and munching quietly.

'Nothing. Forget it.' He backed down again.

In the silence, broken only by the clicking of the wheels on the track as we rushed forward, I could forget nothing. I remembered, as he was obviously remembering, that even now I might be the head of Bradstone Enterprises.

'You haven't told me which of our companies you work

for.' I looked at him thoughtfully. 'We don't have anything in the Third World, yet you seem to know quite a bit about it.'

'That was before I joined Bradstone Enterprises,' he said. 'They—Bradstone—thought my background might be useful.'

'Which company?' I insisted. 'Bradstone Enterprises is the umbrella title, it covers a lot of different interests.

'I know.' He appeared to be thinking furiously. Too furiously. It was a simple question, the answer ought to be on the tip of his tongue. Surely he knew which company employed him.

'Er, well, I'm sort of a floating troubleshooter,' he said. 'I cover all the companies. Whichever one is having a problem, they send me in to deal with it.'

Pretty good. But was it quite good enough?

'And which company is picking up the tab for this little jaunt?'

'At the moment, you are. I'd say it comes under Personal Services, wouldn't you?'

He shouldn't have reminded me that I'd been paying. Bradstone Enterprises was better organized than that. Or was it? Had things been getting slipshod during Buck's last illness? He tried, but there had been many days when he had held the reins in a very loose hand. It would come as no surprise to me to learn that Cousin Everett was not the brilliant administrator he thought he was. I realized that I had better begin checking into the efficiency of the middle management when I got back.

'Sorry about the financial situation,' he said. 'But you rushed off without any warning, didn't you?'

I gave an involuntary nod. So did he.

'Caught us on the hop. I'd just got back from another assignment and had passport in hand, so they turned me round and sent me off with you. I didn't—' the bitterness in his voice gave the ring of truth to the words—'I didn't even have time to turn in my expense account. That's why I'm broke and you're paying—but it won't always be like that. I hope you'll let me take you out and prove that I can pick up a check or two when we get back.'

'It would be a refreshing novelty.' So we were to meet again, were we, after this episode was over? I found that the idea cheered me. I fought against the feeling. One of the first things Buck had ever taught me was that there were an awful lot of men around who would like to marry into Bradstone Enterprises. I had to be as wary as a Crown Princess. I could thank my lucky stars that I had not been born in the era when a husband automatically assumed all rights to his wife's fortune and could proceed to gamble it away or keep other women with it. When the time came, he would see to the prenuptial contract for me.

Only Buck had not foreseen the day when we might all have to manage without him. If he had occasionally had intimations of mortality, he had pushed them away so successfully that he had pushed them out of our minds, as well. Nevertheless, the time had come. I heard myself sigh.

'You're exhausted.' Russ had heard it, too. 'Try to catch a bit more sleep. I'll wake you at Victoria.'

I woke without any help as the train pulled into Victoria Station. Again, the bustle of the departing passengers was like an alarm clock. Doors began slamming before the train had even stopped and the more athletic leaped out and spurted for the baggage trolleys, rolling them back in triumph. The more timorous waited until the train had actually stopped and then dismounted.

People were streaming past our windows and when I saw Jan-Carl stiffen, I looked out to see the Arab women passing. They turned their *yashmaks* away as they saw me look out and went along, presumably chattering earnestly to each other. Jan-Carl gave me an accusing look and reached for his suitcase.

'Just another couple of minutes.' Russ laid a detaining hand on his arm. 'We're in no great rush; we want to see who else might have been on the train.'

'Good idea.' I settled back ostentatiously and watched Jan-Carl mirror my movement, although with an expression that bordered on the sulky. I didn't know what attraction those Arab women had for him, but I did not want him near them again. With any luck, they'd be gone by the time we left the train—on their way to begin shoplifting at Harrod's, as the man had said.

Was that what had given Jan-Carl the idea of pickpocketing? No, of course not, he didn't speak English.

A sudden furtive movement outside attracted my attention. I glanced out just in time to see a vaguely familiar figure dodge behind a column. If he had walked along normally, I would never have noticed, but he had obviously been startled—and rattled—to find himself opposite my window. He was wearing jeans now and a long-sleeved sweater, but he was still carrying the backpack with Canadian maple leaf badges.

'Russ—'

'I saw him. Where's the other one?' Russ craned his neck to look back along the platform. 'No sign of him.'

Jan-Carl looked from one of us to the other, his mood had changed and his eyes were bright and mischievous. I was relieved to see how much he had perked up over the past few hours. Undoubtedly, there would still be times of tears and grief, but he was coping with his mother's death far better than I had feared. The excitement of travel and the increasing distance from the scene had obviously helped. I could pinpoint the start of his recovery from the time we had boarded the ferry and he had realized that we were leaving the European Continent. Now that we were in England, he was cheerier still. By the time we reached home, the onslaught of new experiences would have further buried the unhappy memories. He was probably now looking forward to his first trans-Atlantic jet crossing.

'Okay,' Russ said. Only the stragglers were still meandering down the platform, the elderly who had let the others surge ahead and the heavily-laden who had lost the battle for the luggage trolleys. 'Let's go!'

We were the last through the barrier into the bustle of the station. Overhead, myriad panes of oblong glass turned the roof into a giant mullioned window, supported by Victorian pillars and arches. In contrast, modern fast food centres angled out into the concourse, islands of fluorescent lighting and familiar food. A faint scent of hamburgers wafted towards us.

'Hold on to him,' Russ said as Jan-Carl edged towards the stand.

'Got him!' I caught Jan-Carl's hand and held on tight. If he slipped away from us, he could get hopelessly lost. 'What now?'

'I suggest we feint for the Tube.'

'What?'

'The subway . . . underground . . . to Heathrow. Let's go down and get our tickets. And follow my lead.'

We crossed the concourse and went down a flight of stairs marked by a circle with a bar through it. The downstairs ticket office was busy with the early-morning rush hour. Russ paused to study a wall map with the various routes marked in different colours and showing all the stations.

'Look around,' he said without moving his lips. 'See if there's anyone we know around here.'

'Bingo!' I spotted him at once, lurking by a ticket machine and making great play over searching for the right change. And there were our Arab charmers again. How had they got behind us when they had started out ahead of us?

'That's what I thought,' he said. 'Come on.'

We joined the line at the ticket window and Russ loudly bought one-way tickets to Heathrow for two adults and one child. He collected them, then bent down as though Jan-Carl had just muttered something. He put his ear close to Jan-Carl's mouth so that no watcher could discern whether he was saying anything or not.

'Oh no!' He straightened up with a rueful grin. 'I might have known it! He has to go to the bathroom. We'd better go back up to the station, they've got one there.'

'That's not a bad idea,' I said and received an approving nod.

'We might as well get comfortable,' Russ said. 'It's not as though we're in any great rush. There's an afternoon plane. Maybe we could do a bit of sightseeing first. Have you been to London before?'

'Never. I'd love to see some of it. If we've got a bit of time in hand, let's make the most of it.'

Our eavesdropper was getting a discouraged droop at the thought of trailing us all over the city. The Arab women finished their quiet discussion and melted away in the direction of the underground trains.

Jan-Carl had been jiggling about. Perhaps Russ's bluff was true after all, and he *was* in urgent need of a lavatory.

'Okay,' Russ said. 'Let's go!'

We rushed up the stairs to the station and headed directly for the Ladies and Gentlemen signs. When I glanced back over my shoulder, no one was in pursuit.

'If they're smart,' Russ said, 'they'll go straight to Heathrow and wait for us there. Let's keep them waiting —' He waved his hand at my sign. 'Go in and take your time. We intend to.'

I took my time. I fixed my hair and put on lipstick. I even combed out that wretched wig before carefully storing it back in my holdall. I might need it again at Heathrow in order to pass for Jan-Carl's Scandinavian mother, but for a few hours at least, I wanted to look like myself. Sightseeing could be tiring enough without feeling that you were one of the sights.

They were waiting for me just opposite the door. Russ

was deep in a pink-tinted newspaper and Jan-Carl was wolfing down double-chocolate chip cookies.

'So far, so good.' Russ lowered the *Financial Times*. 'The old boy is still hanging on. If anything had happened to him, this is the paper that would feature the story. Just for good measure, I got the *International Herald-Tribune*, too, and they confirm that the Stock Markets of the world are holding steady. You're okay. You'll get Jan-Carl back in time, after all.'

'All we have to do is get him there.' I looked at Jan-Carl, who was reaching into his bag for another cookie. He looked up at me and offered me the bag.

'Thank you, Jan-Carl.' As there were still several cookies, I took one. Suddenly, I was ravenous with relief. Buck was still alive. I'd be back with him soon. The cookie was suddenly the most delicious thing I'd ever tasted.

Jan-Carl gave me a brilliant smile; he seemed to sense my mood. He jabbered something at me and I nodded. It seemed to be the right response. He pointed up to a couple of pigeons fluttering around the arches of the roof and laughed. I laughed, too. Several of the people around us looked up and did not seem so amused.

'All right.' I caught Jan-Carl's hand and swung to face Russ. 'Where shall we start? Buckingham Palace? The Tower of London? Madame Tuss—?'

'Not this time.' Russ had been carefully surveying the area around us. Now he grabbed my arm and hurried us towards one of the platforms at the end of the station. 'We're not giving anybody a chance to pick up our trail again. We've lost them—for the moment—and we're going to improve that shining moment. We're taking the Gatwick Shuttle. While they're waiting at Heathrow, we'll be on our way from Gatwick!'

'But—' I knew it made sense, yet I could not help feeling a pang of disappointment. When would I be here again? 'No sightseeing at all? Not even the teeniest nearest sight?'

'Another time,' he promised. 'I'll walk your feet off the next time we come over.'

This was the second time he had referred to the future. As though we had one. Together.

'Good. Only a couple in line ahead of us for tickets.' He joined the line and I automatically reached for my money.

'No, this is still on Jan-Carl.' He grinned—yes, very appealingly. 'Your turn at the airport.'

'That's the expensive turn.' That inbuilt caution flickered again. 'You're not so dumb.'

'Almost the last time,' he said. 'I might let you buy me a souvenir. Once we're back in the States and I've collected what's owed me, I'll do some paying. If—' the grin didn't quite fade—'if you ever want to see me again, that is.'

'We'll see.' At least, he had some sensitivity about his position—and mine. But I was the Bradstone heiress, a brilliant catch for a rising young executive in Bradstone Enterprises. You couldn't blame him for trying. 'Meanwhile, will they take American money or should I change some into pounds?'

'Let's get the next shuttle. They'll have a Bureau de Change at the airport. The sooner we get there, the safer we'll feel.'

There was no arguing with that. Jan-Carl and I followed close on his heels as he showed our tickets at the barrier, stuffing what remained of Jan-Carl's largesse into his wallet and shoving it back into his pocket.

The train glided from the station almost as soon as we had seated ourselves and I felt a wave of elation. After all the delays, all the terrors, we were on our way home at last.

The elation continued all the way to Gatwick; for the whole glorious journey, I was completely happy. My nephew was beside me, my . . . friend was sitting opposite us, Buck was still hanging on and we would be with him in just a few more hours. Once again, however precariously, all was right with my world.

At Gatwick, we kept watch until the train emptied, then went up the escalator to the airport. Although it was crowded with people, none of them had anything to do with us. We had successfully outwitted our pursuers—and that, too, was a glorious feeling.

Luck was with us all the way. We picked up standby tickets on a direct flight to Boston leaving in an hour and I cashed in enough dollars to pay for them, with extra left over.

We went directly to the Departure Lounge with time enough to investigate the Duty-Free Shop, prompted by a firm hint from Jan-Carl, who tugged at us until we went in that direction. Russ headed for the Scotch; Jan-Carl tugged me towards the chocolates and toys.

We all met again at the check-out desk. 'I owe you some money, old man,' Russ said to Jan-Carl. 'I'll settle up when we get home, all right?'

As Russ spoke, he pulled out his wallet and something fluttered to the floor. I hardly registered Jan-Carl's happy nod of agreement as I stooped to retrieve it. His business card, I supposed. I could not resist a peek to see just what position he *did* hold in Bradstone Enterprises and in which company.

'Hurry up!' Russ waited at the end of the counter as the girl rang up my purchases and looked at me expectantly. 'Pay the lady and let's get out of here. They're calling our flight.'

'You dropped something,' I said coldly, amazed that I could still speak. Something seemed to have frozen deep within me. I was turned to ice; I could barely move. I dropped the card on the counter between us, face up.

'PRESS' it said.

'You're a reporter!' I snarled. 'A newspaper man. One of *them!* And I was such a fool—'

'Oh-oh!' Russ looked at me uncertainly. 'Look, it's not

what you think. At least, it might have started out that way,
but now—'

'Don't speak to me!'

'*Faster Hope*—' Jan-Carl tugged at my skirt. '*Faster
Hope*—'  .

'That will be twenty-two pounds and seventy-five pence,
madam.' The cashier seemed to think that the problem
might have something to do with my inadequate grasp of a
strange currency.

'*Faster Hope*—' Jan-Carl seemed worried that I might
have changed my mind about paying for his selections.

'Hope, please believe me—'

'Don't speak to me!' I hurled three brown banknotes
down on the counter, scooped up Jan-Carl's bag of purchases
and stumbled towards the passenger loading bay with Jan-
Carl. 'Don't ever speak to me again!'

When I glanced back over my shoulder, Russ was collecting my change from the cashier.

He would!


## CHAPTER 17


'So, that's him.' Ada gave Jan-Carl a measuring look. He
stared back coolly, but with a trace of bewilderment. He
was putting up a brave front, but the bewilderment had
been evident ever since we had left Gatwick.

Part of it was due to the inability to understand why
Russ had suddenly changed from friend to enemy and been
consigned to a seat at the other end of the plane with no
visiting privileges. Even if he'd spoken English, I don't think
I could have explained it to him.

'Well, don't just stand there. Come in.' Ada had been
waiting at the front door as we drove up. I had telephoned
her from Logan to let her know we were on the way.

'How's Buck?' I had asked the question over the telephone, but I couldn't help asking again. It would be so
ironic if anything had happened while we were driving
home.

'Same as last time you asked me and I told you.' She
closed the door behind us. 'How much deterioration do you
expect in half an hour or so?'

'Sorry. I'm afraid my nerves aren't what they were when
I started out. But—' I glanced at Jan-Carl warningly—'I'll
tell you all about it later.'

'No hurry. You're here now.' Ada picked up Jan Carl's
suitcase. 'Is this all he's got or is there more in the car?'

'That's all. We'll have to organize a shopping expedition
in the morning.'

'Afternoon will be time enough. You look as though you
could do with catching up on your sleep. And the child
could do with some feeding up. What do you say, Jan-Carl?'

He gave her a bright, blank smile.

'He isn't likely to say much,' I warned her. 'He doesn't
speak English.'

'Hmmmph! That ought to make for a real interesting
meeting with his great-grandfather.'

'He's a bright child, I'm sure he'll learn rapidly. I'll find
a private tutor and we'll have him ready to start school in
a few weeks.'

Jan-Carl gave me one of his hostile looks. It seemed that
*school* was recognizable in any language.

'We'll just freshen up,' I said. 'Then I'll take him up to
meet Buck.'

'Don't be so impatient. Your grandfather's having his
nap. After dinner will be time enough.' Her face softened.
'You're home now, there's no rush any more.'

'I guess not.' My attempt at a laugh was unexpectedly
shaky. 'I've been hurrying for so long, I'm afraid I've
forgotten how to slow down.'

'It will come back to you. You could do with a nap

yourself, I expect. Both of you. We'll show Jan-Carl his room and—'

'Oh!' Vilma and Everett, hearing voices, had come out of the living-room to see what all the conversation was about. They hadn't expected to find me there.

'You're back,' Everett said. 'Where have you been?'

'And *who* is that?' Vilma looked from Jan-Carl to me, the wildest suspicions flaring in her eyes.

'What's that child doing here?' She turned to Everett for an answer.

'Er, no—' Everett had the abstracted look of someone hurriedly trying to add up years, subtract months, and find an answer that made sense. But he and Aunt Florence had been living here for ten years and he knew that I had never been absent for the requisite number of months. No, I wasn't bringing my little bastard home to roost.

'Whose child is that?' he demanded of me.

'This is Tad's son.' I touched Jan-Carl lightly on the shoulder. 'My nephew. We've just come back from Europe, where he's been living. Say hello to your Cousins Vilma and Everett, Jan-Carl.'

'Tad's son!' Fortunately, Everett did not wait for a response from Jan-Carl, which might have surprised him. 'What's he doing here? Does Buck know?'

'He's come to stay,' I said. 'This is his home.'

'Then—what's happened to Tad?'

'I—I don't know. But the boy's mother is dead . . . quite recently. Look, can't we talk about this later?'

'Don't go badgering her now, Everett.' Ada came to my rescue. 'She's just got back. Give her time to catch her breath. Come along.' She gestured Jan-Carl up the stairs. 'Let's get you both settled before we play Twenty Questions.'

Vilma and Everett stared after us as we hurried up the stairs. Two hundred and twenty questions was going to be more like it, once they'd grasped the full import of the situation. I didn't look back, but I had the feeling that their mouths were still open.

'Well,' Ada chuckled, 'that's set the cat among the pigeons.'

'Yes, and wait until Aunt Florence sees him!'

'Ha!' Ada hadn't been so cheerful since the onslaught of Buck's illness. 'Just wait! She's sick enough already. She's been in bed with one of her migraines for the past two days.'

'What brought it on this time?'

'Temper, as usual. You know how she is when she can't get her own way. For once, Everett's put his foot down and is siding with his wife—and about time, too. Here, Jan-Carl, this is your room. How do you like it?'

The old nursery at the top corner of the house looked out over the side lawns and the sea. I'd always loved the view from the two enormous picture windows and, when the time had come to move out, had claimed the room immediately beneath, so that I still had the same views. They seemed to please Jan-Carl, too. He crossed straight to the window overlooking the ocean and stared out at the horizon.

'I can see we'll have to get out the sailboat when he's a bit older,' Ada said. 'It will be good to have someone using it again.'

'It needs a complete overhaul. By the time he's old enough, it might be easier to get a new one.' I looked around absently, the room could do with a complete overhaul, too; the nursery-rhyme characters gambolling along the walls were a bit young for Jan-Carl. But there was plenty of time to take care of items like that.

'You want a bath before dinner, Jan-Carl?' Ada swung open the door of the *en suite* bathroom with its small bathtub and child-high sink. 'You got plenty of time.'

Jan-Carl wandered in to inspect the fittings; he seemed no more eager than most children to leap into a bath, but his gaze was appreciative. It obviously made him feel quite grown up to have a private apartment. This was more like it, his attitude implied. His faith in me was being restored after having been badly shaken by his first sight of Ada's old rattletrap of a car.

'Jan-Carl, I'm going down to my room. It's right underneath this, on the floor below.' I felt absurd trying to pantomime all this under Ada's amused gaze. 'You'll be all right here for a while, won't you?'

'*Faster Hope*—'He was instantly at my side again, clutching my hand. He'd got the drift all right, and he wasn't going to let me out of his sight.

'All right, come along then.' I couldn't blame him. I was the only person he knew in this house of strangers, in this whole foreign country. I was his one link with the life that was now behind him. I wondered whether Tad had ever told him any stories about his American family. I determined that we were going to find that English-language tutor as soon as possible; that would make life a lot easier for all of us.

'Looks just like his father did at that age.' Ada followed us down to my room. 'I hope he hasn't inherited his—' She broke off as we heard footsteps.

Vilma was coming down the hallway. She gave us a perfunctory smile and tapped on the door of one of the guest-rooms before opening it and going inside.

'Do we have a guest?' I looked at Ada in surprise. The guest-rooms hadn't been used for ages; we weren't very social these days.

'Why do you think your Aunt Florence has taken to her bed? You know what a snob she is.'

Ada obviously felt that this was more of an explanation than I did.

'But who—?' I broke off as a woman's voice floated from the guest-room, loud and belligerent.

'What's the matter with this dress? Ain't it good enough for your classy in-laws?' A familiar voice; I had heard it recently. Very recently.

Incredulous, I ran down the hallway and pushed open the guest-room door. Vilma turned to stare at me in surprise, but it was the woman facing her who complained.

'Don't anybody knock at doors no more?'

'Hello, Irma,' I said. 'What are you doing here?'

'I guess I gotta right to visit my daughter if I want to.'

'I thought you were visiting your other daughter,' I reminded her. 'The one in Belgium. The last time I saw you, you were waiting for your son-in-law to collect you.'

'Yuh, well, I got tired of waiting. He didn't come and there wasn't nobody to talk to after you left. So, I decided I'd visit my other daughter instead.'

Like Ada's explanation, this left a lot to be desired. The only thing that was completely explained was Aunt Florence's retreat into migraine and a darkened room.

'Why, Hope—' Vilma cooed, in excessively genteel tones. 'Do I gather you've met my mother?'

'In Brussels,' I said. 'In fact, we flew over on the same plane. Quite a coincidence, wasn't it?' They must have had to move fast to get Irma on that plane, once I'd decided I was going.

*They?* Everett and Vilma, or Vilma working on her own? I had been vaguely conscious for some time that things in my room were not always the way I had left them, but it hadn't bothered me too much—my life being a depressingly open book. Now I wondered how long and how seriously they had been spying on me. Was it just out of idle curiosity, or was there a deeper motive?

'Yuh, well, life is full of coincidences. They happen to people all the time. I can remember once—'

'Ada said you've been here a couple of days. You didn't wait very long for your son-in-law, Irma.' Because there was no reason to wait, once I'd slipped away from her and she could not pick up my trail again?

'Yuh, well, I guess I'm the impatient type. Besides, it

gives me the creeps hanging around all alone where they
don't speak English.'

'Mother, dear—' Vilma advanced and closed her hand
over Irma's arm, warning her to silence. 'Hope has just
arrived and she must be tired. We can all have a good talk
over dinner.'

'Suits me.' Irma retreated several steps. 'See you later.'

'Yes.' I needed time to consider things, too. How had
they known where I was going? I'd told only Ada and Buck.
Then I suddenly remembered writing down the address of
the *Poisson d'Or* on the notepad on the desk. I'd torn off the
page and taken it with me—but the impression of my writing
would have remained on the next sheet for anyone to find.
I hadn't realized they were watching me so closely.

'Yes, we'll have a long talk over dinner,' I promised as I
closed the door behind me.

'Huh! That ought to do wonders for everybody's diges-
tion!' Ada was agog and making no pretence that she had
not been hanging on every word. 'What are they up to?
Nothing good, I'll be bound.'

'I don't know,' I said wearily. I had thought it was all
over, now I found myself tense and suspicious again.

Jan-Carl felt it, too; he seemed to have retreated into
himself. Like a shadow, he trailed us back to my room and
again was drawn to the window, this time the one that
looked out over the side lawns. He stared out wistfully.

'Do you want to go out and play, Jan-Carl?' It struck me
as absurd, even as I asked. I had never seen Jan-Carl
playing; I wondered if he knew how. 'Perhaps you can go
out tomorrow—or the next day.'

I went over and stood behind him at the window. The
lawn was still green, but the autumn foliage was in full riot
of colour. Even as I looked, a gust of wind swept in from
the sea and a flurry of leaves lifted lazily from the trees
edging the lawn and began swirling earthwards.

Jan-Carl pointed to the brilliant trees and said something.

'You don't have colours like that where you come from,
do you?' I assumed that was what he had been pointing out.
'Those are sugar maples, that's why the leaves are so red.
There are lots of maple trees here—'

*And in Canada.* In fact, it was their national emblem. I
had a sudden vision of a backpack with the maple leaf
emblem. Was that what Jan-Carl had really been pointing
out? Did the maple leaves convey something more to him
than vivid beauty?

They would to me from now on. I shuddered.

'What's the matter?' Ada had been watching.

'Nothing,' I said. 'Nothing I can explain right now. I—
I'm overtired. I think I *will* rest for a while.'

'Told you so!' Ada said triumphantly. 'Both of you need
a rest. I'll see to the boy—' She began urging Jan-Carl
towards the door.

'Yes, and Ada—'

She turned back inquiringly.

'Stay with Jan-Carl. Don't leave him alone.'


# CHAPTER 18

'I think you're crazy,' Artie said. 'You know that, don't
you?'

'You've made it very clear,' Russ said. 'Just keep driving.'

'She doesn't want to see you again. She'll have you thrown
out. Thrown out?—You'll never get in!'

'This is the turn-off, isn't it?' Dim memories of that
long-ago vigil came back to Russ. 'Just follow the road along
and we'll come to the gatehouse.'

'And we'll stay at the gatehouse! I don't know why you're
even bothering.'

'I told you. I owe her money.'

'That reminds me—' Artie swerved on to the private shore road. 'You owe me money, too.'

'You'll get it. Better switch your headlights on.' The sun had disappeared abruptly and it was growing dark. There were so few lights along the road that the sound of the incoming tide crashing against the rocks on the other side of the sea wall was a better guide to their position.

'She hates you,' Artie insisted, 'and I'm not surprised. You know how these stinking rich snobs feel about publicity anyway.'

'I know. The old social rule still holds: "A lady gets her name in the newspapers only three times in her life: when she is born, when she marries, and when she dies."'

And she sure as hell didn't want any newspaper reporters around when she was bending the law just as far as it could bend without breaking.

Too bad Hope had to be a Bradstone. For the first time in longer than he could remember, he'd been attracted to a young, eligible woman of his own nationality. Even the prospect of a desk job in Boston had begun to look less like a living death. There might be compensations.

And she'd been interested, too. He couldn't have been mistaken about that. Even though she'd thought he was the worst kind of Company Man, and a fortune-hunter to boot, she had been beginning to respond.

If only he could have had more time before she found out. Better still, if he had told her himself . . .

'I'm talking to you—' Artie had a right to be annoyed. He'd had other plans for the evening when Russ had commandeered him and his car.

'Oh, sorry. I was . . . thinking. What did you say?'

'I said, "What's wrong with this picture?" The one straight ahead. Look hard. What do you see?'

'Nothing.' Russ frowned at the gatehouse just ahead. 'That's funny, there's no one there . . . and the gates are open.'

'Exactly.' Artie slowed the car. 'The last I heard, the old guy was taking so long to die they thought it might be another false alarm. So they drew straws for a skeleton crew. There was one local man, one stringer for the Press Association and a couple of TV camera crew standing by. Now there's no one here.'

'And the gates are open,' Russ repeated thoughtfully. 'That could mean that it's all over—or it's just beginning. If they're rushing him to hospital, they'd have left the gates open so that the ambulance wouldn't be delayed. And the skeleton crew would have followed them up to the house.'

'We go ahead?'

'We go ahead,' Russ said. If the worst was happening, Hope would need him—whether she admitted it or not.

Artie drove cautiously up the narrow, winding drive, ready to brake instantly if he found an ambulance hurtling towards them. But their progress was unchallenged and, when they reached the porticoed entrance to the big house, there was no sign of other vehicles or any activity. Lighted windows gave no indication of disturbance within.

'Pull up over by the bushes,' Russ instructed. 'We'll take a look around before we go in.'

'Why don't you include me out?' Artie grumbled. 'I'm just along for the ride.' Nevertheless, he got out and closed his door silently.

The wind was sweeping in from the sea, the damp chill of it betokening the advancing frosts. Just a few more weeks and they would be into winter. This place must look beautiful in the snow.

'Some layout.' Artie was trying not to be impressed. 'You want to return money to this dame? Why? She doesn't need any more.'

'It's the principle of the thing.' Russ skirted the lawn, peering into the darkness of the trees and shrubs of its border. Not that he could see much; the moon only appeared fitfully from behind clouds and a sea mist was beginning to roll in. The rustling of the bushes might be due to the wind, falling leaves, or small night creatures. There could not be any dogs guarding the estate or they would have been baying by now.

There was a stone terrace on the seaward side of the house with French windows, slightly ajar, giving on to it from one of the rooms. The terrace was deserted; white-painted iron patio furniture lay about like bleached skeletons; someone must have removed their cushions to preserve them from the damp night air.

Russ glanced over the railing and saw that there was a sheer drop to the rocks below. Instinctively, he knew that was too much like Luxembourg for Hope's comfort right now; it was undoubtedly someone else who had been domestic about the cushions.

A figure appeared at a lighted window in the room above the terrace. Russ moved back against the slightly-open French window, pushing it farther open and catching a glimpse of the library it led into. After a moment, the shadow —he had an impression of a nurse's cap on the head— silhouetted on the flagstones of the terrace moved away. He glanced over his shoulder into the library; from somewhere beyond it, he could hear voices approaching.

'Artie?' He moved rapidly. He was already in Hope's bad books; it would not improve the situation if she caught him trespassing. 'Let's go round to the front and ring the bell.'

'Fine with me.' Artie, who had been lurking at the far end of the terrace, fell into step beside him. 'What do you think's happened to the skeleton crew? Think a more important story has broken and they've been called away?'

'Possibly.' Russ had an uneasy feeling that would not go away. He identified it as part of the letdown after excitement, the adrenalin still flowing but with no action looming to channel it into. He wondered if Hope, too, had this hangover from too much happening too fast.

'They aren't expecting company,' Artie remarked. The

light by the front door was dark, indicating that the family was in for the night and no visitors were anticipated.

'Then we'll surprise them.' Russ rang the bell and they waited. He was about to ring it again when an overhead light went on and they could feel themselves being scrutinized from some hidden spyhole. After an indecisive interlude, the door opened a few inches.

'What is it?' a female voice demanded.

'I'd like to see Miss Bradstone,' Russ said. 'Miss Hope Bradstone.'

'Maybe you would—but would she like to see you?'

'Why don't you ask her and find out? Tell her it's Russ.'

'Russ who?'

'Russ—' He could not remember the surname he had used. 'Just tell her it's Russ. She'll know.'

'Will she?' The door shut again in their faces.

'Not very welcoming, are they?' Artie grinned. 'I can see your fame has spread.'

'Come along to the study.' After an interval, the door re-opened. 'You can wait there. Miss Bradstone will be with you when she's finished her dinner. She's just started.'

They entered and followed a tall, gaunt woman down a dimly-lit hallway and into the room Russ recognized as the one that opened on to the terrace.

'Sit down,' Ada said. 'It will be some while. Do you—' her tone discouraged the idea—'do you want a drink?'

'Well, since you insist,' Artie said.

'Later, perhaps.' Russ overruled him.

'Suit yourselves.' Ada shrugged and left the room.

'Nice place they've got here.' Artie looked around. 'Too bad about the servants.'

'I'm not sure she's a servant,' Russ said. 'If that's Ada, her position is equivocal, to say the least.'

'You mean she knows where the body is buried, so they can't fire her? I'd say—'

'Be quiet a minute, will you?' Russ raised a silencing

hand and listened. He had caught a blurred murmur of argumentative voices coming from somewhere behind a booklined wall and there was a growing hum of machinery.

'This place gives me the creeps!' Artie turned apprehensively to see what Russ was staring at behind him.

A section of the bookcase slid aside and an ancient man in a wheelchair glared out at them. 'Who are you?' he demanded.

'Now, Mr Bradstone—' A nurse pushed the wheelchair out into the room and the elevator door closed behind them, the bookcase moved back into place. 'You promised me you wouldn't get excited. You know I don't approve of this. It won't do you any good.'

'Shut up, Helen!' Having obviously won the battle in order to get this far, the old man's order was perfunctory. He glared at Russ and Artie. 'Well?'

'Good evening, sir.' Russ stepped forward but decided it was more prudent not to offer his hand—it might get bitten off. 'I'm a friend of Hope's. We travelled from Brussels together.'

'Did you?' The sharp eyes took in his every detail, but judgement was suspended. 'Where is she?'

'Still having dinner, I believe. Miss—Ada said she'd be along shortly.'

'Did she?'

'Yes, she did.' Russ bit back his annoyance. The way these old Yankees answered every question with another question was one of the things he had forgotten about New England, but he was getting a refresher course now.

'Mr Bradstone—' The nurse risked her luck again. 'Why don't you let me make you more comfortable? You can stretch out on the sofa and—'

'No, damn it! I'm not going to have my great-grandson's first memory of me be of an old man in bed. This—' he struck the arm of the wheelchair angrily—'this is bad enough!'

That was Buck Bradstone—true to his tradition—in there and fighting to the last. Russ felt reluctant admiration. You had to hand it to the old boy.

'What are you grinning at, you young fool? And who's that other one? Is he a friend of Hope's, too? What's he doing here?'

'Don't look at me,' Artie said. 'I'm an innocent bystander. I'm just along for the ride.'

'Mr Bradstone—you're getting excited.'

'Shut up, Helen, and go and fetch the family. I don't care whether they've finished their dinner or not. I'm not going to sit around here all night!'

'Yes, Mr Bradstone.' The nurse flounced off, her huff modified by the prospect of being able to be rude to the family in her employer's name.

Buck Bradstone leaned back in his wheelchair and closed his eyes, breathing slowly and carefully.

'Are you all right, sir?'

'Friend of Hope's, are you?' The eyes opened again, fixing Russ with a sharp, suspicious gaze.

'Yes, sir. Whether she believes it or not.'

'Like that, is it?' A wintry smile twitched the thin lips. 'She always did have more of a temper than she let on.'

'Yes, sir,' Russ said ruefully. 'She still has.'

'And you—' He was not going to get away with it so easily. 'You did nothing to get her dander up?'

'She, er, misunderstood something. That is, she wouldn't let me explain. If I can just talk to her . . . in private.'

'You'll wait your turn! You've seen her more recently than I have. And you've . . . got more time.' His eyes closed again.

Russ shook his head as Artie started forward anxiously. The old boy was just conserving his strength. When you couldn't end a conversation by getting up and leaving the room, cutting everyone off by closing your eyes to them was the next best option.

A chill wind swirled into the room from the half-open French windows, stirring the draperies. Buck Bradstone did not appear to notice. Perhaps he no longer felt the chill, or perhaps he was beyond the point of noticing minor discomforts.

Voices and footsteps outside snapped Buck back to attention. He sat straighter, eyes open, still carefully controlling his breathing; gathering his forces for a major effort.

A man and a woman entered the room first, crossed directly to the wheelchair and kissed the old man on the cheek.

'It's good to see you downstairs again, Uncle Buck,' Everett said. 'You must be feeling better.'

'Well enough, well enough.' The thin murmur belied the words.

'We're so pleased—' The woman looked at the next person entering and lost the thread of her comment. 'Mother,' she snapped, 'I told you to wait in the dining-room.'

'What's the matter, ain't I good enough to meet your uncle-in-law? Besides, I hate to eat alone.'

'And you seldom do,' Russ said. 'Hello, Irma.'

'You again! You following me around, or something? How did you get here?'

'I drove him down.' Artie took the question literally.

'And who the hell are you?'

'I'd introduce you,' Russ said, 'but I don't think you'd appreciate it.'

'You bet I wouldn't!' She turned away.

Buck had been following their exchanges with moderate interest, but his gaze kept returning to the doorway. At last, the child he had waited so long to see stood there.

'Don't be shy—' Ada nudged the boy forward. 'Go and say hello to your great-grandfather.'

Jan-Carl advanced hesitantly into the room, trying not to stare too openly at the man in the wheelchair. His surprised gaze encountered Russ and he smiled tentatively, then looked back over his shoulder to find Hope and determine what his reaction should be.

'Oh!' Hope stopped dead. 'What's *he* doing here?' She turned on Ada furiously. 'I told you to send him away! I don't want to see him.'

'He's come all this way,' Ada said practically. 'Can't do any harm to be civil to him.'

'Who says it can't?' Irma was always ready to weigh in on a good fight. 'He's after her money.'

'*Au contraire*,' Russ said. 'I came here to give her some.' He held out a blue banknote and some coins. 'You forgot your change at Gatwick.'

'I don't want it,' Hope said stiffly. 'You've wasted your journey—and your time.'

'That's telling him, honey. Give this kinda creep an inch and they take ten miles. He'll start by giving you money— but wait until you see how much he takes from you.'

'Mother, please!'

Hope might not want the money, but Jan-Carl was displaying no such inhibitions. He crossed to Russ quickly and took the money before he could change hs mind.

'Look at that!' Ada crowed. 'He's a chip off the old block, all right. *Your* old block,' she added to Buck. A faint intimate smile flickered between them.

Jan-Carl looked at Hope uncertainly and offered her the money.

'Keep it!' she snapped. 'I don't want it!'

'Please—' Nurse Helen's face had flamed with jealousy at Buck and Ada's intimate moment. Now, starchy and officious, she tried to exert her authority again. 'I must insist that you stop all this arguing. I can't have my patient excited.'

For once, Buck did not try to shut her up, although his eyes narrowed. He waited and watched.

Jan-Carl shrugged and pocketed the English money, then

turned his attention to Buck again. They stared at each other gravely.

'Well, what do you think of it all?' Buck demanded. 'Think you'll like it here?'

'He doesn't speak English,' Hope said quickly. 'I'll start looking for a tutor Monday.'

'Doesn't, hey?' Buck was still speaking directly to Jan-Carl. 'Why not? You're a big boy. Are you stupid or just lazy?'

Jan-Carl's lips tightened, he looked pleadingly towards Hope.

'His mother was Swedish,' Hope rushed to explain.

'And his father was American. *Was.*' Buck glared at Hope. 'Did you find him?'

'No—' Hope glanced around at her relatives, all listening avidly. 'I'll tell you all about it later.'

'She didn't have that kid in Brussels,' Irma offered helpfully. 'She musta picked him up in Luxembourg. That's where she *said* she was going.'

'It seems you've had quite a trip,' Buck said. His gaze returned to Russ with a question in it.

'It was very . . . hectic,' Hope said.

'And you've brought back my great-grandson, who doesn't even speak English.'

'I wouldn't worry about that, sir,' Russ said. 'I think you'll be amazed how quickly he picks it up after one or two lessons.'

'It ain't a hard language,' Irma said. 'I don't see why everybody don't speak it. It's a lot easier than that French.'

'You may be right,' Buck answered them both impartially, his thoughtful gaze returning to Russ again. 'I'd be interested to hear your rationale.'

Jan-Carl had retreated, step by wary step, until he was close to Hope. He reached for her hand.

'I'm perfectly willing to let you hear it,' Russ said. 'But

I agree with Hope. I think we should have our discussion in a bit more privacy.'

'There are entirely too many people in this room,' Nurse Helen said briskly. 'You're exhausting Mr Bradstone. And you know what *that* means,' she added darkly. 'He'll have another of his bad nights.'

'Artie,' Russ said, 'why don't you take Irma for a walk around the garden.'

'If he's a friend of yours, I ain't going nowhere with him!'

'Vilma,' Everett said quietly. 'Suppose you and your mother go back to the dining-room. Perhaps Mr . . . er, Artie, would like to go with you and have coffee. In fact, Ada, how about coffee for all of us?'

'Good idea,' she said. 'Nurse Helen can make it.'

'I can't leave my patient!'

'Oh yes you can. I'll take care of Buck. I've been looking after him for a lot longer than you have. Matter of fact, Everett, why don't you go along with her and help carry the tray when she's ready?'

'But I—' This was not what Everett had intended.

'Go along, Everett,' Buck ordered.

Buck was still master in his own house and no one quite dared to disobey him. The library seemed colder and more spacious when they had all unwillingly left it.

'Now then . . .' Buck relaxed. Ada stood behind him, one hand lightly resting on his shoulder. 'Let's hear it.'

'I think Hope should start—' Russ looked at her and broke off.

Hope had suddenly gone rigid, her eyes wide with horror, staring at something behind him.

Russ turned slowly. The French windows were wide open and the man they had last seen in London was standing there. He no longer had his backpack.

This time, he held a gun in his hand.

# CHAPTER 19

'Just be quiet,' the man ordered. 'Don't try to be a hero or the kid gets it.'

Jan-Carl's grip on my hand tightened, although he didn't make a sound. He realized that the word *kid* meant him—and there could be no mistake about where the gun was pointing.

'You—the skinny old bag!' The muzzle swerved briefly in Ada's direction before returning to Jan-Carl. 'Lock that door! We don't want the others interrupting us.'

In speaking to Ada that way in front of Buck, he'd made an enemy for life—which, if Ada had any say about it, wouldn't be for long. In a smouldering fury, she stalked across the room, slammed the door and locked it noisily.

'That's better.' He seemed nervous, as well he might, facing all of us. If it weren't for that gun, he wouldn't stand a chance. Already, Russ was manœuvring for a better tactical position. I tried to slide Jan-Carl behind me, but he was resisting.

'Stop that!' I wasn't sure whether he was speaking to me or Russ; we both froze.

'You were staying at the *Poisson d'Or*—' I decided to adopt the theory that attack is the best defence. 'What are you doing here?'

'I'll ask the questions—and the kid had better answer them. Where is he?'

'Jan-Carl doesn't speak English.' I was conscious of Ada's pale face as she watched Buck, who seemed to be breathing with more difficulty. Although he hadn't reached a critical stage. Not yet.

'Who are you?' Buck struggled to command the situation. 'What do you want?'

'The kid knows.' The man took a menacing step forward. I wondered how I could ever have thought of him as an innocent hiker. He was all thug now. A thug . . . a racketeer . . . a deserter . . . an associate of Tad's.

Inga's murderer.

'Okay, kid, where is he?'

Jan-Carl shrank back against me.

'Why don't you put that gun away?' I tried to stay calm and reasonable for Jan-Carl's sake. 'We can talk more sensibly.'

'You can't use it anyway,' Russ pointed out. 'The minute you fire, everyone in the house will come rushing back. They'll break the door down, if they have to, and you'll be outnumbered.'

'That's right.' I thought Russ was taking an optimistic view of Everett's capabilities, but I was sure that a locked door would not stand for long between Nurse Helen and her patient. Irma would probably be worth two of Everett, as well. We had started on our talk before Buck's summons interrupted our dinner and I knew I had nothing to fear from Irma. Vilma had telephoned her to speculate on the reason I was rushing off to an obscure hotel in Brussels and, having nothing more important to do, Irma had decided to go along and keep tabs on me. She might be irritating and nosey, but there was no real harm in her. Unlike the man facing us with the gun.

'Where is he?' The man repeated his question to Jan-Carl. The gun did not waver. One shot would be all he needed. What good would it do to overpower him after Jan-Carl was dead?

'The boy doesn't speak English,' Buck said. 'If you'll tell us who you're looking for, one of us might be able to give you the information.'

'I want Tad.'

'Thaddeus Bradstone is dead.' Buck's face was grim and slowly greying. I measured the distance between me and

the cabinet where the spare oxygen cylinder was stored. A
quick sprint—

'Dead? When? I don't believe it!'

'Thaddeus Bradstone has been dead for the best part of
twenty years.'

'Maybe he has to you, grandpa, but I can tell you he's
been alive and messing up my business for the past five
years. I've got a score to settle with him.'

'Haven't you done enough already?' I couldn't hold it
back any longer. 'You killed Inga!'

'One down—and two to go.'

'Jan-Carl hasn't done anything.' Again I tried to thrust
him behind me and he resisted. 'He's too young to even
know what's been going on.'

'What *has* been going on?' Russ was a reporter to the last.
The over-casual way he spoke would have alerted anyone
used to the Press to the fact that anything they said would
be quoted at length.

'He moved in on the sweetest little racket going and—'

'And broke it up!' I felt a glow of triumph, for a moment
the chimera of my Returning Hero flared again.

'Hell, no! He took it over!'

'What was it?' Russ was hot on the trail. 'Drugs?'

'Safer than that. Who needs all the drugs hassle
when there are easier ways to make a fortune? They
hand it to you on a plate over there. All you need are
a few big trucks loaded with legitimate cargo and
lots of duplicate paperwork. Just keep them moving
from one EEC country to another; picking up subsidies
as they leave one country; getting more subsidies as
they enter another country. Neat, clean—and practically
legal. You just forget to unload and keep them on the
move.'

'Common Market Fraud!' I remembered the newspaper
headlines I had seen in Brussels. 'The newspapers were full
of it over there.'

'And then the bastard killed my partner! Threw him off the ferry! I'd only turned my back for a few minutes.'

'You'd thrown Inga off the bridge.' Two wrongs might not make a right, but I couldn't feel any sympathy for a murderer who'd been repaid in his own coin. 'But Tad wasn't on the Ferry. I'd have seen him—'

I caught my breath. Dark shadows were stirring beyond the French windows. I looked away, so that I wouldn't alert our captor. I felt Jan-Carl's hand slip out of mine.

'That still doesn't give you any quarrel with Jan-Carl.' Russ had glanced at me and now began to move forward, creating a diversion. He wasn't sure what was happening, but he knew I wanted attention drawn away from the terrace. Had we established such a rapport in such a short space of time?

'Stand still! I told you not to move!' The gun moved to cover Russ. I felt my heart lurch uncontrollably.

Buck's breathing was increasingly laboured. Disregarding the command, Ada bent over him anxiously.

'Don't anybody move! I'm leaving now and I'm taking the kid with me. Don't worry, he'll speak English when I get to work on him. Come on, kid—' He gestured with his gun. 'Get moving!'

'Not my great-grandson!' Buck's head snapped up; he clawed at the wheels, trying to charge at the man in his wheelchair, but Ada was holding it firmly.

'It's all right, Buck.' I had risked another look at the French windows. The black shadows had materialized into solid forms, unexpected forms. I watched incredulously as the two Arab women, *yashmaks* still in place, strode forward and took up positions behind the fraudster.

'*Pappa!*' With a glad cry, Jan-Carl sprang forward and hurled himself into the arms of one of the Arab women. '*Min pappa!*'

The other Arab woman wrapped her arms around our former captor, one massive hand at his throat, the other closing over his hand with such force that he dropped the gun.

Russ dived for it, then came to stand by my side. He held the gun uncertainly as he stared at the scene before us.

'I take it these are friends?' he asked.

'Oh yes.' I leaned against him, suddenly limp with relief. Tad had detached Jan-Carl and moved to help his friend. Between them, they had the gunman bound and gagged in seconds. It looked like a practised routine, one they had used before. I didn't want to think about that.

'Why the Arab costumes?' Russ was still curious. 'I thought it was traditional to dress as nuns for this sort of thing.'

The larger man released his hold on his captive and let him slump to the floor. He pulled off his *yashmak* to reveal a beard.

'Ah yes, I see,' Russ murmured. 'Not exactly the right accessory for a nun's habit, but it did very well for the absent-minded professor.'

'You were at the *Poisson d'Or*, too!' I recognized him now.

'Inga shouldn't have sent you there.' Tad's voice was muffled. 'We'd taken it over as our headquarters, but she didn't know.' His voice hardened. 'I tried to keep all that away from her.'

'Tad, please—' I gestured weakly.

'Sorry.' He reached up and slipped off the *yashmak*.

'Hmmmph!' Ada said. 'You haven't changed much.'

She was right. How could I have imagined that I wouldn't know him? It was the old Tad, only a bit older, a few wrinkles, more . . . careworn.

'You mean my life of wickedness hasn't left its mark on me?' He gave the sudden wicked grin. 'Ah, but you should see the state of the portrait hidden away in the attic!'

'Thaddeus!' It wasn't quite the thunderous calling-to-order of old, but it was a creditable attempt. I wondered if

Tad realized how ill Buck was; he wasn't showing much sign of it now.

'Hello, Buck.' They faced each other. I wondered how I could ever have hoped for a reconciliation. They were too much alike. And now Tad had gone beyond the pale. He was no longer someone who had merely given in to weakness or fear; he was a declared outlaw.

'You haven't changed, Buck.' Neither had Tad, essentially. He was still a Bradstone. Still Buck's grandson. Still my brother. How had it all gone so wrong?

Russ's arm tightened around me. Until then, I hadn't been aware that that faint muffled sob had come from me.

'*Faster Hope—*' Jan-Carl had heard it, too. He hurried to my side. '*Jag tycker om dig, faster Hope. Jag . . . älskar . . . dig.*'

'Oh, stop that!' It was unfair to take it out on the child, but I did. 'You don't have to pretend any more. We all know you can speak English!' Something I should have remembered a long time ago came back to me. 'Your mother taught English. And you have an American father. Of course you speak English!'

'Hope. *Fas*—Aunt Hope. Do not be angry with me. Please.' He lifted his arms to me. 'I . . . I love you. I . . . want to . . . say goodbye . . .'

'No!' I caught him up in my arms and faced Tad. 'You can't! What kind of a life would he have? No mother and—'

'And a crook for a father,' Tad finished for me.

'Is that it?' Buck glared at Tad. 'Have you come to take the boy away? She's right, you know. You have nothing to offer him.'

'Oh, I don't know. I've been building up quite an empire of my own. Not an honest one, perhaps, but the Bradstone blood runs strong. I've discovered I have quite a talent for organization and administration. I've acquired quite a fortune in my own right.'

'That's where Jan-Carl got all that English money on the

ferry.' Thank heavens, he hadn't stolen it; he wasn't a burgeoning pickpocket, after all. 'You gave it to him!'

'That's right.' Tad gave me an amused glance. 'You weren't doing so well at keeping up with the currencies. I didn't want my son to land in England penniless.'

'Tainted money!' Ada snorted. ''And you know it. It will never do you any good. You'll take that boy away with you over my dead body!'

'You know you're safe, Ada.' Tad gave her a wry grin. 'Maybe if Inga were still alive—' His face hardened. 'But when they killed her, they changed everything. Jan-Carl is better off here.'

'No, Pappa! No!' Jan-Carl rushed back to him. 'I go with you. I stay with you. Please!'

'Be a good boy, Jan-Carl. Take care of your aunt. Although—' his eyes crinkled as he looked from me to Russ —'it may not be for long.'

'I'm glad to see you've still got some sense,' Ada said.

'Oh yes,' Tad agreed. 'There's only one person I'm taking away from here.' His glance flicked to the inert form at his feet. 'And I don't think you'll miss him.'

'What are you going to do with him?' Russ asked.

'Don't answer that!' Suddenly I remembered who Russ was; what he was. 'He's a newspaper reporter. It will be in all the papers—' I pulled away from Russ's restraining arm and moved over to stand beside Buck and Ada. 'He's a traitor in our midst. And I brought him here. I'm sorry.'

'Take it easy,' Tad said. 'It's not the end of the world.'

'But it wasn't all my fault—' I glared at Ada. '*You* let him in. I told you to send him away.'

'That's right,' she said. 'But you didn't see the way your face lit up when I told you he was here.'

'Oh!' I wanted to scream, to spit, to cry. 'And you're going to write about it, aren't you?' I turned on Russ in a fury.

'It's my job.' He met my eyes steadily. 'And it's a great

story. If I don't write it, someone else will. By the way—'
he looked at Tad—'would you mind telling me what you've
done with my colleagues? I understand there were several
of them at the gatehouse.'

'Oh, them. They're all right.' Tad shrugged dismissively.
'We trussed them up and put them in the greenhouse. It's
up to you whether you release them before you file your own
story or—' he grinned conspiratorially. 'Or afterwards.'

'Tad!' He was downright encouraging Russ.

'It doesn't matter now, not too much. Call it my wedding
present to the groom.' He grinned at Russ. 'Just one thing
—do you think you could give me twenty-four hours head
start?'

'I think that could be arranged,' Russ said. 'My colleagues
may not be too anxious to rush into print with the information that they were set upon and overpowered by two
Arab women. Their editors might check their expense ac-
counts for bar bills too closely after that one.'

'That's that, then.' Tad nodded to his friend, who scooped
up the bound man and carried him through to the terrace.

'Tad!' The terrace, the sheer drop below! Terror para-
lysed me. 'Tad, you're not going to—?'

'No, not here.' Tad was grimly amused. 'I have other
plans for him. Besides, I wouldn't leave a dead body on
your doorstep, so to speak. He's going with us.'

'Where?' Russ still dared to ask.

'Who knows? That will depend on him.' Tad had the
bland, excessively innocent expression he had always used
when lying. I knew the killer's fate was already sealed. I
avoided Russ's eyes, lest he know it, too.

'Goodbye, Jan-Carl.' Tad hugged his son, as though for
the last time, then pushed him away. 'Stay with Hope. She'll
take care of you.'

'I will,' I promised. 'But, Tad—'

'Well—' He faced Buck. 'I won't ask for your blessing
but . . . would you shake hands with a dead grandson?'

Buck stared at him implacably.

'Go ahead, you old fool—you know you want to!' Ada grabbed Buck's hand and extended it. He did not fight her.

'Too bad it couldn't have been different.' Tad grasped the hand gently. 'But you got your own way, after all. I'm a fighter . . . a killer. Only it's in a private war. At least I'm not killing innocent bystanders.'

'Take care of yourself, damn you!' Ada threw herself on Tad and kissed him on both cheeks. 'And you know what they say—' She sniffed. 'If you can't be good—be careful!'

'Hope—' Tad held out his hand to me. 'Will you walk me to the door?'

'Tad,' I said, as we left the light behind and moved into the shadows at the end of the terrace, 'what's going to happen?'

'Why, we're all going to live happily ever after.' His voice was mocking. 'Don't you know that?'

'Tad, I'm grown up now.'

'You'll be all right. So will Jan-Carl.'

'And you?'

'Too many questions,' he said. 'But you're right. Life has become too complicated. It may be time to bow out gracefully.'

'Tad! No!' I clutched at his arm; I never wanted to let go. 'You don't mean that. You can't!'

'Don't worry, I won't.' He was laughing at me again. 'That's why I wanted to get you out here alone—to warn you. Don't believe everything you hear. And, if you hear my body has been discovered somewhere, don't do anything sentimental like bringing it back here to the family plot. Let them bury it in the local Potter's Field.'

'Tad!' I didn't want to believe I could understand what he was saying. 'Tad, you—'

'The Common Market authorities have been closing in for some time. They've just appointed a special Fraud Squad of their own. The party's over—and it's time to look around for greener fields.'

'Honest fields?'

'I wouldn't guarantee that. I don't know any honest people any more. In any case, it doesn't matter. Thaddeus Bradstone is just about at the end of a short and undistinguished career. The *Poisson d'Or* was always something of a firetrap, you know, but Madame has it well insured. You mustn't be too shocked if you hear some day soon that it's burned down—and the body found in the debris is identified as mine.'

'Tad!' As surely as he had spelled it out, I knew what was going to happen to the gunman he was taking away with him. 'You couldn't! You wouldn't!'

'He killed Inga.' The merciless chill in his voice turned him into a stranger. 'We're the same general height and build. A good session with my dentist and—'

'Tad—don't! For your own sake, please don't.' I stepped away from him in sudden revulsion. He had changed more than I ever could have believed.

'Hope! HOPE!' It was Ada's voice, high-pitched and shrill with panic. 'HOPE!'

'*Buck!*' I knew what must have happened. Buck had seemed so strong, so improved in this past hour. If any of us had stopped to think, we would have known it couldn't last.

'I'm coming, Ada,' I called and, forgetting Tad, turned and ran back into the house.

Russ was pulling the oxygen cylinder out of the cabinet. Ada was bending over Buck, trying to control her tears. The door was open and I could hear footsteps running along the hall. Jan-Carl burst back into the room, Nurse Helen on his heels.

'I knew it!' she snapped. 'I told you he was getting too excited. What have you been doing? I never should have left him.' While she scolded, she did the necessary things with the oxygen cylinder and mask. With the mask strapped over Buck's face and the cylinder hissing, she checked his pulse and stepped back.

'I'm calling an ambulance,' she said quietly. 'We need the paramedics.'

'You're not taking him to the hospital—' Ada raised her tear-stained face in defiance. 'This is his home. This is where he wants to . . . to . . .'

'I'm not sending him to the hospital,' Nurse Helen agreed. 'There isn't time.'

When I went out on the terrace later, much later, for a breath of air, Buck was still hanging on, but expert opinion was that he wouldn't last until morning.

I looked out to the dark horizon, telling myself that he would have preferred it this way. One last burst of activity, in the centre of the excitement, with a sort of reconciliation with his grandson and his great-grandson safely under his roof.

'Hope?' Russ uncurled himself from one of the loungers.

'Oh!' I stifled a cry. 'I thought you'd gone. Long ago.'

'Artie went. I'm still here.'

'I—I'm glad.' His arms closed around me and I tried to shut out all sounds, all thoughts, but they kept intruding.

'Oh! Those poor people tied up in the greenhouse . . .'

'They're okay. Artie set them free. And he couldn't tell them anything because he didn't know anything.'

'Like Inga . . .' But it hadn't saved her.

His arms tightened comfortingly; he didn't say anything.

Then I identified the sound, the deep familiar soughing from the rocks and sea beneath us. I leaned against him and wept quietly.

The tide was going out.

**THE END**